JENNIFER GLADEN

Souled

First published by Valentino Publishing 2020

First edition

ISBN: 978-1-7356987-2-4

Editing by Darcy Werkman
Cover art by Junior's Digital Designs

This book was professionally typeset on Reedsy.
Find out more at reedsy.com

Dedicated to my family and friends who always believed in my vision for Souled

CHAPTER 1 - The Transport

When twelve-year-old Ethan Bradford heard the knock at the door, his heart quickened, and he bounded down the stairs. He skidded through the kitchen, using the doorframe to stop himself in his tracks. He swung open the door and lifted the shoebox-sized package off the porch.

"It came!" He placed it on the kitchen table and ripped open the package. He dug deep through the plastic bubble wrap until his fingers rested on a smaller box. "Finally," he mumbled under his breath. He pulled the box out and held it in front of him like it was the savior of the world. He stared at the picture of the red headset. Not just any accessory, it was the Transport—the one of a kind item specifically designed for the ever-popular video game Seeker.

Ethan grinned as he read the slogan on the front of the box: "Transport - Get in the game." In smaller lettering underneath, he read, "Another viral game by Tinim Inc." Oh yeah. He was ready!

He snapped a photo, texted it to Brody, then added: *My Transport came!*

Same. Max just told me Seeker's already rated number one.

Right? Ethan responded. *I'm dying to download it.*

Can you even imagine? This game is gonna rule.

Yep. I can't wait to see the Seeker Map. It's supposed 2 b a huge fortress.

And I love that you need a key to move on.

Speaking of which, let's check in with Alyssa and Jason and get started.

Ethan put his phone in his pocket and brought the Transport to the living room. Placing it on his head, he unfolded the microphone that was neatly tucked behind the ear cushion and pulled down the tinted plastic visor. He was careful not to push too hard on the sensors across it. Then he fumbled around with the headset, trying to get it in a perfect position, moving it from side to side, up and back until it felt perfect. The ear cushions felt like fluffy clouds surrounding his head. Instantly, all outside sound vanished.

"Woah." Ethan removed the headset and stared at it in awe. He could see why they called it the Transport. This would help him concentrate on the game when Maggie would distract him. He loved hanging out with his sister, who was only a year younger than him, but she talked All. The. Time.

He placed the headset back in the box and grabbed his cell phone to message Alyssa, Jason, and Brody. His phone wasn't the newest version that everyone else had, but it still did the job.

With excitement he could hardly contain, he messaged Alyssa and Jason. *It finally came. I got the Transport.*

Yaaay, Alyssa responded. *Watch out world. Team Dynamite is here.*

Aww yeahhh, Jason chimed in. *Let's get this thing started.*

Ok, Ethan typed. *Let's all download the game, get set up and I'll meet you guys on there. Say 15 minutes?*

It took Ethan much less than the fifteen minutes he allowed himself. He was the founding member of the gaming club, after all. He and Brody often set up the lab for the club's monthly gaming parties. They'd have to have a Seeker party next. It would be easy to plan since he lived down the block from Brody. In fact, Brody popped in and out of the house like anyone in Ethan's family would. Sometimes he'd call Ethan's mom, "Mom."

Ethan slipped on his new headset, set up his new account, and logged in to Seeker. He adjusted the microphone and tested it out to make sure it was working.

A window popped up: *Set up your avatar now.*

Ethan scrolled through the endless list of images, but nothing resonated with him. As if the game read his mind, another window popped up: *Or upload your own image.*

Ethan clicked *Upload* and chose his favorite picture. It was of him standing in front of the lab at school, arms crossed, during the gaming club's first gaming party. His blonde, wavy hair accented his green eyes. It was one of his happier moments since his dad went missing. He still wasn't sure what had happened to him. To be fair, he and Maggie were young children. All he knew was one day everything was normal—the way it always was—and the next, his dad was gone and everything changed. It was as if he disappeared without a trace. Ethan's mom was heartbroken.

Ethan shook his head and pushed the thought of his dad out of his mind. He uploaded the picture and saved it. Another window popped up: *Find Your Friends and Create a Team!*

He uploaded his contacts and quickly found Alyssa Caldwell, Brody Watson, and Jason Graser. Jason typed his name as "Jason Gr-AY-zer," and Ethan had to laugh. Every first day of school, the teachers butchered his name. He got anything from "Grasser" to "Greaser." He even got "Grassier" one time. That was epic. But he was cool about it. It didn't seem to bother him, at least as far as Ethan could tell.

Within minutes, he connected with his friends. He knew Alyssa created the team when he saw "Team Dynamite!!!" because the extra exclamation points were totally her. She was enthusiastic about things and always had been, even when they met in kindergarten. He loved that she wasn't afraid to show him a different perspective on things—and she was usually right. In fact, she was the first person he had told about his dad. He smiled as he thought about their friendship and of how she had given him a hug and promised she would always be there for him. She had told him that he would be okay. His stomach did a quick flip at the thought. He shook the memory from his head and joined the team before more memories could distract him further.

"Alright, let's do this," Ethan said into his microphone.

Brody, Jason, and Alyssa laughed. "Let's do this," all three of them answered.

CHAPTER 2 - The Guardian of Bailiwick

Ethan clicked on the play button. Instantly a swooshing noise surrounded him. At the same time, the image on the screen twisted and spiraled until it was completely black. The blackness seemed to surround Ethan until the screen brightened slightly, and when it did, something was different. Everything looked so . . . real. Did the headset have some sort of 3D or AI feature? He looked around and squinted through the darkness. Within minutes, three other figures appeared.

"Guys," Ethan whispered, "is that you?"

"Yoooo," Alyssa squealed, turning to see everyone. "What is going *on*?"

"Oh, nothing," Jason said sarcastically and waved his hand. "This is totally normal."

"It's as if we really are right in front of each other." Brody waved his hands in front of Ethan.

Ethan pushed Brody's hand away. How could he even do that? This was definitely a new gaming experience. "These headsets really are one of a kind," Ethan said.

"Only the best," came a voice from the darkness.

Footsteps echoed throughout the hall until a tall, thin boy

about Ethan's age appeared.

Who was that? He didn't remember adding anyone to their team.

"Welcome, Team Dynamite," the voice continued. "I'm Drake Knightson, Guardian of the Bailiwick Fortress." Drake waved his arm to the side and more light filled the room. He wore a red T-shirt covered with a leather jacket combined with dark blue jeans and black boots. His black hair was thin and long, reaching below his ears. Hanging around his neck was a gold chain with a plate that read "Guardian of Bailiwick."

He pulled out a scroll and read, "Lord Nith Erikki needs a warrior team to assist him in guarding his fortress. The chosen team must display strength, courage, loyalty, and bravery."

"Oh yeah." Jason pumped his fist in the air. "We got this!"

Drake turned toward him with a stern look and Jason gulped in response. Drake turned back to his scroll. "Your quest is simple. Compete with other teams to secure this fortress. Destroy the obstacle in each room of the fortress to seek out a key. The key allows your team to move on to the next room. The more rooms you secure, the more points you get. Each team is limited to four rooms per twenty-four hours. However, many teams can barely secure one room at a time. Only one team can be the true Seeker."

"Wow," Jason said. "Sweet intro!"

Drake eyed Jason, who quickly moved to the opposite end of the group.

"Follow me inside." Drake moved forward and disappeared in the darkness.

"Ready?" Ethan asked.

"I am if you are," Alyssa said with a smile.

Jason and Brody nodded.

Ethan might have paid attention to the stomach-flipping he felt in response to Alyssa's smile, but what was happening around him stole his full attention.

He took a deep breath and followed Drake into the darkness. As they walked, the darkness faded and a large castle-like structure loomed into view. When they got close, they paused and scanned the scene. Behind Ethan and his friends was a moat with a wooden plank bridge. *Funny,* Ethan thought, *I don't remember crossing that as we made our way over here.* The squared-out walls were formed from grey rectangular stones that surrounded the property.

Brody pointed above and behind the wall where a tall tower stood. "Amazing. This looks so real."

Drake's eyes clouded for a minute. "Yes, I suppose that is the point. Come." He motioned for them to follow as he opened the large iron door. The door creaked and they crept inside.

"Unreal." Alyssa gasped. "Look at all this."

She pointed all around the room, and Ethan stood equally impressed. The inside reminded him of a modern castle. A bright-red rug graced the gold-toned tile floor. The second story walls had large arches lined with gold all around the perimeter with a glittering five-tiered chandelier hanging from the center of the ceiling. The ground level walls had arched doorways aligned perfectly with the arches above them. Finally, Ethan's eyes rested on the elegant stairway across the room, where curved marble railings gently hugged the sides of the stairs.

Drake waved his arm. "Welcome to the Great Hall. Your team gathers here before you enter your level each time you arrive."

"No offense, Mr. Drake," Jason said, and Ethan covered

his face with his hands. Whenever Jason said, "No offense," someone usually got offended. Jason pointed back out of the door they came through. "But back there you said we had to defeat someone in every room. If my house looked like this and I battled in every room, my parents would absolutely freak!"

Drake turned to him. "This is *only* a game, is it not?"

Jason shrugged. "I'm seriously starting to wonder."

Brody nodded. "It feels like we're actually here." He pinched himself. "Ouch! And we are carrying on a real conversation with a game bot."

Drake eyed Ethan and Brody. "It really is another level of AI."

Ethan exchanged an excited look with Brody. They were just talking about this in the gaming club at school. They anticipated something cool when Seeker was released, but this was beyond anything Ethan imagined.

Drake continued. "Now, throughout the game, you will have opportunities to collect tools to help you through. I recommend you snag and keep *all* of them. Some of your quests won't be survivable without them." He waved his hand, and a digital inventory appeared above them. There were several greyed-out shapes, and the rest of the boxes were empty. "These are the most helpful tools." Drake pointed at the greyed-out items: a ring, a sword, a large jug, and keys. "But as I said, I recommend you keep everything you find or earn." He snapped his fingers and the large jug in the inventory lit up. "Everyone starts with a large jug of water. These will be found throughout the game. They get used up quickly, so grab them when you see them." He waved his hand again and the inventory disappeared.

"Good luck," Drake said and began to walk away. He stopped and turned back to the group. "Oh, I forgot to tell you. You cannot leave the game without saving your progress." Drake pointed to a tall, round chamber to the left side of the grand stairs.

The group walked over to the glass chamber and pressed the *Open* button. Fog seeped out around them as they walked inside. There were several marbleized countertop stations all around the walls of the chamber.

Ethan held his hand over the *Save* button and hesitated. He looked at his friends and they all paused along with him.

"On three?" Alyssa asked.

Ethan took a deep breath. "Yeah. Let's do this."

"Let's do this," all three responded.

When Brody finished counting to three, everyone pressed the save button. A sharp prickle pierced inside Ethan's head. He reached up and massaged his temples, which reminded him of the headset he was wearing. Light swirled all around them followed by a computerized voice. "Process Saved."

"Did you guys feel that?" Ethan asked.

His friends shifted uncomfortably, but then Alyssa nodded.

Without warning, his head jerked. "What was that?" he asked the others.

They stared at him.

He felt a hard tug on his head. "You guys don't feel that?"

"No." Alyssa shook her head.

The others shook their heads as well.

"Someone—"

His voice was cut away, and the last thing he saw was his friends rushing towards him.

CHAPTER 3 - Consumed

The room went dark and swirled. When the spinning finally stopped, Ethan looked around at his new surroundings and realized he was right back in his living room. When he looked up, he saw his sister, Maggie, holding his headset with a look of horror on her face.

Ethan pointed to Maggie and said, "What the . . . how'd you—"

She dropped the headset to the ground and clasped her hand over her mouth.

"Careful with that." Ethan went to pick it up, but Maggie moved in and hugged him. He hugged her back and asked, "What is it?"

Maggie backed away. "Are you okay?"

"Yeah," Ethan picked up the headset and dusted it off with his shirt. "Why?"

"You were out of it!"

Ethan laughed, wringing his hands nervously. "What do you mean? I was playing my game."

Maggie shook her head. "When you twist your hands like that, you're nervous about something."

He opened his mouth to argue, but when he looked down, he realized she was right. Instead of admitting it, he avoided her eyes and picked up the headset. He took it over to the gaming console and set it down carefully on the rack that came with it. Just then the side door to the kitchen opened and their mom walked through, groceries in hand.

Maggie frowned, still concerned about Ethan. "It really was strange. It was like you were here, but you were not here."

Their mom laughed. "Ah, Maggie," she said as she placed the groceries on the counter. "Welcome to the gaming world."

Ethan rolled his eyes.

Maggie's face turned red and Ethan knew what that meant. That was the first warning sign that Maggie was about to erupt. He often did the same thing. "You don't understand." She pointed to Ethan. "I was calling his name—*screaming* it even. He had no idea what was happening around him"—Maggie pointed to the headset—"until I ripped that thing off him."

Ethan smiled. "It's okay, Maggs. It's a new game, and I must have been really into it."

Maggie didn't look convinced, but she thankfully dropped the subject.

Their mom unpacked the groceries and started to fill a pot on the stove. As she did, she said to Ethan, "I'm assuming you didn't start homework yet."

Ethan shook his head. But who could blame him? The headphones were right there just moments after he got home from school. "I'm on it," he said and dashed off to his room.

* * *

Ethan, Alyssa, Jason, and Brody gathered the next morning at their usual meeting spot for their daily walk to school. The stop sign at the end of his block worked best for everyone since they all lived within a few blocks of each other. During the summer, they spent the days going from one house to another.

Alyssa nudged Ethan as they began their walk.

"What was that for?" He rubbed his arm for effect.

"What the heck happened to you yesterday?" Alyssa asked as they approached an intersection. She folded her arms while they waited for a line of cars to pass.

"What do you mean?"

"In the game," Brody said. "You disappeared after we saved."

After the last car passed, they all stepped into the street. "Yeah, it was weird," Jason said. "Your avatar looked like it was being pulled and twisted. That didn't happen to any of us."

Ethan stuck his hands in his pockets. "I assumed that everyone disappeared from the game after we saved."

"No," Alyssa said. "We tried to stop you, but we couldn't get to you in time."

Ethan remembered how they all reached out to him right before Maggie grabbed his headset . . . His thought trailed off and his heart sank. Was that the difference?

"Woah," Brody said, breaking Ethan's chain of thought. "You look like you saw a ghost."

Ethan and his friends rounded the corner and their school appeared down the block. He shook his head. "What was it like for you guys when you got off the game?"

Alyssa, Jason, and Brody exchanged looks, which told Ethan their experience was not the same as his.

"Uh, we . . . exited the game," Brody said. He scrunched his eyebrows and reached for Ethan's forehead. "You sure you're okay, man?"

"Yeah." Ethan pushed Brody's hand away. "It was strange. One minute I saved the game and the next—"

The morning bell blared just as Alyssa opened the door to the school, giving Team Dynamite just minutes to make their way to class.

As Ethan reached his first class, he remembered he forgot to do his science homework. Fortunately, his first period was Study Hall. He sat in his usual seat and began to work. He did okay until he got stuck on question four. *Maybe I should ask Max where to find the answer*. Max always had a knack for science. He looked over three rows where Max usually sat, but his seat was empty. It looked like Ethan was on his own for this one. Then, a few minutes before the end of class, Max walked in, covering a yawn with one hand and holding a late slip with the other. He handed the teacher the note and sat behind Ethan.

"Ugh," Max groaned. "Why does school have to start so *early*?"

Ethan shrugged, then gathered his books. "Late night last night?"

Max yawned and nodded. "Yeah, I got my Transport headset yesterday. I was on *forever*."

"Lucky," Ethan mumbled. "First, my sister interrupted me. Then my mom made me do my homework." Ethan waved his paper in the air.

Max grinned. "Looks like you missed one."

The bell rang as both boys laughed, and they gathered the rest of their books.

During lunch, Ethan, Alyssa, and Brody grabbed their usual table. Ethan sat on one side of Alyssa. He had an apple on his tray along with a generous helping of cheese-covered fries. Alyssa crinkled her eyebrows when she saw his tray.

Ethan grinned. "Hey, at least an apple is healthy, right?" Then his smile faded as he showed Alyssa a scrunched-up piece of paper. "My mom is going to kill me." He ran his fingers through his blonde, wavy hair. "Mr. Bently must hate me. Can you believe he gave me a demerit?"

Jason shot Ethan a you-must-be-kidding look as he approached the table with his tray. "What do you expect?" He grabbed a chair and sat between Alyssa and Brody. "For Mr. Bently to ignore the fact that you didn't have your homework done?"

Brody laughed. "You should talk! Weren't you missing Math?"

Alyssa sighed. "And I got *nothing* done."

Ethan nodded. "Well, at least we're all in the same boat."

"Yeah, and it's not only us," Brody said. "I don't know about your class, but we spent the first fifteen minutes in English sitting there while Ms. Carrol wrote out demerits."

Everyone nodded in agreement.

As the rest of the day crawled by, Ethan's mind filled with worry. *What will Mom say when I get home?* He could forget about concentrating in class. When the final bell rang, he grabbed his things and slowly made his way home. When he arrived, Ethan was relieved to find out his mom was not getting home until later, even though it prolonged the trouble he knew he was going to get into. But at least he would get a little time on Seeker before then. He threw his backpack down in the hall and went straight to the living room and picked up the Transport. He was about to put it on his head when he heard the front door slam.

"Ethan!" his mom's voice boomed as she came into sight. "Hold it right there, mister."

CHAPTER 4 - The Library

Ethan's stomach dropped. Everything in him wanted to flee the room.

She held her phone in the air. "I got a notification from school." She walked over and put her purse on the counter. She turned to Ethan, pointing the phone at him as she talked—well, yelled. "I thought I told you last night to get your homework done."

Ethan shuffled his feet. "I know. I'm sorry. I—"

"Oh, no you don't."

Ethan was pretty sure her face couldn't turn any more red.

"No more excuses. You've had this game one day—one day—and you're getting demerits for not finishing your work."

"I did the rest of it," he tried.

"Uh-uh. Not good enough. Instead of gaming, you are finishing last night's work and doing today's. It looks like no Seeker tonight."

Ethan frowned. "But—"

"No 'buts,'" she interrupted. "You have a lot of work to do."

"But Brody, Alyssa, and Jason are going on later. I promised I'd be there."

Mom shook her head and pointed to the coffee table.

"Then you better get busy. The only way you're getting on

tonight is if everything is finished."

"Okay, okay, I will."

"Now." Mom pointed again to the coffee table, then held out her hand for the game controller. She started to walk away and turned back to face Ethan. "Let me warn you now. If you let this game interfere with your schoolwork again, you will be *grounded* from it." Ethan cringed. With that, she stalked into the kitchen.

Three and a half painstakingly long hours later, Ethan closed the last homework book. Finally done. He glanced at his watch. 7:30. He rushed over to his phone.

what time r u all getting on 2nite? he sent in a group message.

There u r, Brody replied. *We've been waiting 4ever.*

Oh good, Alyssa's message rang in. *I was beginning to worry.*

long story, Ethan sent. *u guys ready?*

They all replied with a resounding *yes*.

OK. Let's do this. He put on the Transport and glanced at his phone to see Team Dynamite reply, *Let's do this.*

A few minutes later, everyone met in the Great Hall.

"Welcome back," Drake greeted them.

"Wow." Jason pointed around the room. "Look how many people are playing now."

Ethan took a few steps forward and glanced around. Jason was right. There were avatars with their teams all around them. Players were scurrying all over the room, heading in different directions. He watched as one team headed for the chamber before logging off.

"Definitely more than last time," Ethan agreed.

Alyssa turned to Drake. "So, where do we start?"

Drake motioned them to follow him. "Be careful," he said as they arrived at the first doorway on the right-hand side of the room labeled LIBRARY. "Some levels you need strength—" He paused as Jason stood, held up his arms, and dramatically mimed bicep flexing. Drake sighed. "But most require smarts." He looked back over at Jason, who shrugged, then at the rest of the group.

Ethan and Brody grinned at each other. Jason was smart, but he loved to joke around a lot. Ethan had to admit it definitely helped destress uncomfortable situations. Besides, Jason was always more focused after kidding around. Jason once said it was as if it cleared out negative emotions and thoughts that clouded his thinking. He once compared it to the blue sky after a thick cloud lifts.

Drake pointed to the gold-plated number above the library sign. "This is level one. You must secure the key to defeat the level. In this level, laser rings are supplied to assist you on your mission. Everyone good so far?" When everyone nodded, Drake continued. "Good. Once you have the key, you can move on to the next level."

Ethan opened the doorway and his team followed him in. The walls were several stories high and lined with shelf after shelf of books. However, it was the medium-sized dragon standing in the room's center, guarding the credit-card-shaped key, that stopped Ethan in his tracks. The dragon also happened to be blocking their exit.

In the corner of the room, there was a dark mahogany desk. A sign placed in a large, diamond-covered frame sat in the front. The sign read:

SECURE THE LIBRARY BY RECOVERING THE KEY FROM THE DRAGON.

Brody lifted the sign and looked behind it. "Get the key? How?" He rummaged through the desk.

Ethan made his way over to the dragon and circled her. The dragon mirrored his movements. Ethan moved his gaze down to the floor and saw the golden key glowing by the dragon's feet. Ethan squatted down and inched closer, but the dragon reared up on her hind legs and roared.

"Yo," Brody called. "I think I found something!" Brody held up four metal rings, each with a ruby stone on the front.

Everyone rushed over, earning another roar from the dragon.

Alyssa paused. "Careful, guys. She doesn't like sudden movements."

Brody picked up a ring. "These must be the laser rings." He put one on his finger, held it in front of him, and aimed it toward the wall. A laser shot out and Brody fell back in surprise.

Jason ran over and shook his head. "Amateur." He helped Brody up and then pointed his ring in front of the dragon. As a laser shot out, it just missed the dragon's foot. The animal roared and swung at the lasers coming her way. She paused and stared down Jason while she pulled the key closer. Jason leapt backwards.

Brody stifled a laugh. "Yeah, that was much better."

Jason folded his arms across his chest and smirked. "It was better than falling back on my butt." He rolled the ring between his fingers and turned serious. "I'm not sure if these things will do the trick."

Brody lifted his ring. "Drake said we needed laser rings . . . and here are the laser rings."

Alyssa chimed in as well. "Why else would they be in here?" Alyssa picked up a ring and held it next to the ring on her pointer finger.

"I love how this matches my grandmother's ring that I always wear."

"Well, to answer your question"—Ethan picked up his ring—"maybe it can be helpful in other ways." With a grin, he aimed it at the dragon. The dragon moved into a defensive stance. Ethan shot the laser, purposefully missing the dragon. "That's not what we have to do at all."

"Am I the only one who knows how to shoot?" Jason asked and took another aim. He stood in a you-won't-get-by me-this-time stance.

"Stop!" Ethan grabbed Jason's arm. "I'm saying there may be another way to defeat the dragon."

Alyssa glanced at all the books around the room. "Maybe there's something hidden in the books. We *are* surrounded by a lot of information."

Everyone looked around the room. Ethan eyed the wall-to-wall book collection.

"Yeah, you have fun with that," Jason said with a smirk.

Alyssa smiled and shrugged.

"Watch," Ethan said. He moved closer to the dragon and then circled it. Once again, the dragon mirrored his movements. "The dragon is copying me. See?"

He moved in a circle a third time, and the dragon copied. Alyssa moved closer and held her hand out in front of herself. The dragon copied her movements.

"Can we get her to move away from the key?" Brody asked.

Jason crouched to the ground, and the dragon did the same. "Probably. Ethan, I think you're on to something." Jason stood. So did the dragon.

"Aww, she's actually cute," Alyssa cooed. Everyone looked at her. She cleared her throat. "For a dragon."

Jason continued moving around and lured the dragon to face away from the key. The dragon stopped when she realized how far away she was and leapt back over. "Okay," Jason said. "I'm pretty sure we all knew it wasn't going to be that easy."

Brody nodded. "We still have these laser rings." He put one on his finger and aimed at the dragon.

"No." Alyssa jumped between him and the dragon. "Don't you dare!"

"What?" everyone shouted in unison.

Alyssa shook her head. "What I mean is, keep trying to distract her. Chase her away from the key with the laser ring. We can lure her a little bit away from the key—"

Brody nodded. "And then scare her so she moves even further away. Good thinking, Alyssa."

"So," Jason asked as he looked at each person, one at a time, "who would like to be the dragon bait?"

Everyone stared at each other in silence. Alyssa shook her head and sighed. "Oh, I'll do it. Really, guys." She smiled teasingly.

Then, she moved closer to the dragon. She held out her hand. The dragon imitated her. Alyssa sat. So did the dragon. Alyssa stood and took a step. The dragon stood too but didn't follow her.

"Too much, too fast?" Alyssa asked out loud.

Ethan smiled at how Alyssa was with the dragon. She had to be scared, but she was still able to keep the dragon calm. It was as if it was starting to trust her.

"Hmm," Alyssa said and looked at Ethan. "Do we have anything to offer her?"

"Offer?" Ethan repeated.

Alyssa nodded. "Maybe she'll be less hostile if we have

something to give her."

"What about one of the snacks from our inventory," Brody said.

Alyssa waved her hand in the air and the inventory appeared. She pulled out a loaf of bread. She showed the bread to the dragon and took a few steps forward. This time, the dragon followed. She dropped a piece of bread. The dragon picked it up, then gave a happy fluttering huff in response.

"Aww, guys." Alyssa tilted her head.

"If you coo over that thing one more time," Jason said, shaking his head.

Ethan and Brody looked at each other and laughed.

Alyssa took another few steps forward. The dragon followed again and Alyssa gave her more bread. Once again, the dragon gave a happy huff. "I'm going to call you Flutter." She offered Flutter another piece of bread.

"Flutter?" Jason shook his head. "Aaaaand now she's naming it."

Brody pointed to the key, which was now completely uncovered on the floor. "It's open."

Brody crept slowly over to the key and snatched it up. "Got it. Let's go."

Alyssa inched toward Ethan. When she was close enough, Ethan grabbed her hand and they joined Brody and Jason at the door. Flutter glanced at where the key was and roared. She launched at the group, but Alyssa stood in front of her friends, arms outstretched. Flutter came to a halt when Alyssa offered her another piece of bread. Flutter hesitated, eyes still fixed on the key in Brody's hands. Alyssa pushed the piece of bread closer to Flutter. Flutter looked at the bread and then back at Alyssa. When Alyssa nodded, Flutter accepted the treat.

"You can have this whole thing"—Alyssa waved the loaf in the air over her head—"if you let us leave with that key." Alyssa lowered her head to look directly into Flutter's eyes. Flutter gave a slightly annoyed huff but slowly backed away from the group. Alyssa smiled. "Thank you, Flutter." She bent down and gently put the rest of the bread on the ground. She slid it to Flutter, then stood. Flutter bowed her head, then took her treat.

"Now, who has the key?" Alyssa asked.

Brody held it up. Alyssa nodded, and Brody pressed the key against the card reader. Instantly the door slid open and Jason, Alyssa, and Brody ran out of the room. As Ethan followed, a jug of water appeared at the door. Ethan grabbed it. When the door closed, he waved his hand in the air and the inventory appeared. The laser rings and the new jug of water levitated toward their spots, which lit up once they landed inside.

"Not bad for beginners," Drake said as he appeared next to them. He then fell into step with them as they made their way to the chamber. "You had a whole other approach than I did."

"You play—"

"Shhh." Drake held his fingers up to his lips, interrupting Alyssa's question. "Never mind. He'll hear us. I shouldn't have said anything."

"Okayyy," Brody said.

Ethan was barely paying attention to the conversation. As he made his way down the hall, he saw something move out of the corner of his eye. He turned his head and saw a shadow move at the end of the left side of the hall. He glanced back at his friends who were way ahead of him now, but his curiosity got the best of him. He pulled away from his group and cautiously walked to the end of the hall, but he saw no one. As he turned around, there was a tiny doorway hidden in the corner. Ethan stepped closer to find a white door with a tiny red sign that said RESTRICTED ACCESS. A window sat in the top section of the door. It was just out of range for Ethan to reach it, so he stood on his tiptoes to peer through.

While blinds were blocking most of his vision, he was able to make out some details. The room had silhouettes of several computers resting on long tables. A closer look inside showed that the rows of computers were all working at the same time—like a network of computers Ethan would find in the tech lab at school.

Ethan craned his neck to see if he could make out anything else. That's when a dark figure in a black rugged cloak rushed through the room. Ethan pulled back and pressed himself flat against the wall next to the door. He peeked again, this time to see the figure standing right in front of the door. He pointed to Ethan. *Drake never said this was part of the game,* Ethan thought. He backed away from the door as the door handle jiggled. His heart pounded. What the heck was that? Could it have been that shadowy thing he saw earlier? But something bothered him even more. Even though they were just in a game, whatever that thing was, Ethan was pretty sure it was now looking for him. The door handle jiggled again, and he was not going to wait to see if that creature was successful. He turned and darted away as fast as he could. As he raced toward his friends, Alyssa clasped her hand against her face.

CHAPTER 5 - Seeker's Pull

"Are you okay?" Alyssa asked when he reached her. "You look terrified." She moved away from the chamber and placed her hands on Ethan's shoulders. His heart rate seemed to slow to a more normal pace.

Ethan glanced down the hall. He was relieved to see that the figure from the secret room had not followed him. Ethan shivered and tried to shake away the creepy feeling that lingered inside him. "Yea." He cleared his throat. "I think so." He joined the rest of his friends in the chamber. The usual fog seeped outside and he made his way to a station at the rounded marble countertop.

"You look like you saw a ghost," Brody said as Ethan settled in. "Are you okay?"

"Um . . . yeah," Ethan said as he stumbled over his words. He thought about what he saw earlier. Maybe it was just his imagination running wild. *Anything could have created a shadow in that room . . . right?*

Alyssa tilted her head. "I know you better than that. What's up?" She rested her hands on her hips.

Ethan tried to think of the right sentences to tell his friends about the shadow in the window. Instead, he said, "I . . . just . . . I saw . . ." He pointed to the door behind them. "Someone saw me," he blurted at last. "And he was not like the other characters running around. He looked directly at me . . . and pointed."

Everyone's eyes widened.

"This shadowy figure. It was there. It saw me." He swallowed hard. "When our eyes met, he pointed at me. I think he tried to leave the room to come after me, because the doorknob was jiggling so much I thought it would fall off." He shrugged the creepy feeling away again. "I'm not sure what it was. Maybe I overreacted. Maybe it was some bonus to the game."

Ethan tried to convince himself as much as his friends that it was no big deal. He pushed that nagging and alarming feeling deep down inside. He pressed the save button and once again felt the prickle in his head. Then, he exited the game. Even though he was away from the game, and even though he was trying to convince himself and his friends that what he saw was nothing, he still couldn't shake the uneasy feeling lingering inside him.

Worse, when he was back in his living room and looked at the clock, it said 12:00 AM. There was no way he was on for that long. He ran into the kitchen and opened his school laptop to check the digital time. 12:00 AM. He ran his hand through his shaggy blonde curls. He didn't know how it happened, but he had been on the game for four and a half hours.

Beep, beep, beep, beep! Ethan's alarm clock blared a few hours later. He groaned and rolled over in bed.

"Let's go, Ethan! You're going to be late for school," his mom called from the bottom of the stairs. It seemed like it was only a few minutes since the alarm blared, but one look at the clock told him it was much longer than that. He pulled the covers over his head in response. How was it morning already?

His bedroom door creaked open. "Ethan," Maggie whispered from the door.

He lifted his head to see Maggie's blonde head poke through the opening.

"Mom's going to freak if you don't get up soon. I figured I'd give you a heads up."

He smiled. "Thanks for having my back, Mags. I owe you one." If his mom found out how late he was on the game last night, that would be the end of Seeker. He'd have to be more careful.

A half-hour later, Team Dynamite met at the corner. Ethan rubbed his eyes. "Man, I'm beat." He looked at each of his friends who appeared just as tired as he was.

"Yeah, I am soooooo tiiiirrrred," Alyssa said and leaned against the stop sign. "Did we really play until—"

"12:00 am," Brody interrupted. "Yep, that's the time I got last night." Everyone nodded in agreement. Brody tugged on his blue shirt that was only half tucked in as they all started their walk to school. "I slept so late that I didn't even change clothes."

Alyssa crinkled her nose at the thought and glanced at Ethan.

Ethan laughed and then ran his hands through his unruly curls. "Good thing Maggie got me up this morning. My mom freaked out last night because I missed some schoolwork. I'd probably be grounded from the game forever if she knew how long I'd been on."

"Yeah," Jason said. "Speaking of which, what about that person freaking out in the lobby? Did you hear any of it?"

Ethan shook his head.

Alyssa perked up. "Yes, what was that all about?"

"I couldn't make out what he said," Brody added. "But

whatever it was, that dude was aaaannngry."

"Angry doesn't even begin to describe it," Jason said. "He was yelling, kicking, screaming."

"It couldn't have been that bad. I didn't hear anything," Ethan said. "Besides, I can totally relate to being frustrated with a game." He thought about War Zone—a shooter war game. Someone used a hack that made him immune to shots. He shot at Ethan's character, who tried to shoot back, but it had no effect. The next shot his opponent took knocked him out of the game. Ethan felt his face flush the thought.

"Uh-oh." Jason put his arm around Ethan's shoulders. "Ethan's thinking about his 'Test the Durability of the Controller' challenge."

Ethan rolled his eyes. "He cheated. He used one of those immune-to-shots hacks. Besides, I didn't mean to throw it." He faced the ground, afraid to look at anyone. "It just slipped."

Ethan and Jason smiled at each other.

Brody rested a hand on Ethan and gave a supporting smile. "I don't think the controller did well in the challenge."

Jason laughed. "Yeah, it was a total fail."

Ethan straightened and eyed Jason. "Anyway. Max was on there yesterday. I'll see if he knows anything. See if there's something we should watch out for."

Later in Study Hall, Max was nowhere to be found. *Probably late again,* Ethan thought, but something stirred in him that made him uncomfortable as he kept looking back at the door. When the bell rang, he caught up with Alyssa who had class down the hall.

"I'm worried about Max," Ethan said as he fell into step with her. "He's never out. Late? Sure. But rarely out."

Alyssa nodded. "You're right. But he could just be sick. Try to relax a little." She sent him an encouraging smile.

A wave of warmth hit him, easing some of the worries he had. "Maybe," he said.

As he made his way through the day, he decided Alyssa was right. After school, Ethan intended to get his homework done before getting on Seeker, but everyone on Team Dynamite planned to meet online right away. He knew it was a bad idea, especially if his mom found out, but there was something about Seeker that he couldn't resist. He picked up his controller and the Transport to prepare for the game.

"Mom is going to kill you." Maggie's accusing voice made Ethan jump. He almost dropped the Transport as his heart leaped into his throat.

"Geez, Mags, don't sneak up on me like that. You scared me to death."

Maggie rolled her eyes. "That will be the least of your problems. You know Mom wants us to get schoolwork done before this stuff." She pointed to the controller in Ethan's hand.

"I know." Ethan gritted his teeth. Irritation bubbled inside him. He wanted to play without her nagging him, but he took a deep breath and softened his tone. "I won't be on long."

Maggie glared at him.

"I swear." He held his left hand up. "We're just playing for a little bit, and then I'll get to work. I'm already late meeting them as it is."

Maggie eyed him, and she didn't look convinced.

"In fact," Ethan continued, "I'll be off so fast that I'll be done with this, finished my homework, and have it put away before Mom even walks in the door."

Maggie frowned. "What about dinner?"

"What do you mean, 'what about dinner?'" *Why is she wasting so much time?*

Maggie flipped her hair behind her shoulders and threw her hands on her hips. "We're supposed to make dinner tonight since Mom will be a little late."

"Ohhhhh, right." He looked longingly at his gaming console. "It's just that I promised to meet everyone right away."

Maggie scowled. "Oh, never mind. I thought we could do this together to hang out a little, but you obviously have other plans."

Ethan frowned and put his controller down. "I'm sorry, Maggs. I'll help if you want me to." He meant those words, but he also glanced back at the controller, and he still had the Transport in his hand. He was supposed to meet everyone in a few minutes, and the pull of the game was so strong.

Maggie shook her head and frowned. "No, go play. I see how much it means to you."

"Maggs—"

"No, really, it's fine." She walked away and held her hand in the air over her head.

CHAPTER 6 - The Billiard Room

"What took you so long?" Alyssa asked as soon as Ethan entered Seeker. Brody, Jason, and Alyssa were already there.

He sighed and quickly told everyone about what happened with Maggie.

"Anyway, where did this epic freak out take place yesterday that you were telling me about?"

Jason pointed. "It was outside of Room Three."

"Ahh, I see Team Dynamite has returned," Drake called from across the other side of the Grand Hall. He walked over and joined the group. "I couldn't help but overhear you talking."

Ethan gave a sideways glance to Brody. *Overhear? How can a bot "overhear"?* He turned his attention back to Drake. *But then again, everything about him is so realistic—the way his hair moves when he turns his head, how he feels a breeze when someone walks past him.*

"That 'freak out,'" Drake continued, "was another player. One who was overconfident."

"Overconfident?" Jason asked. "He sounded pretty ticked off. That didn't look overconfident to me."

Drake frowned. "That's just it. He was angry because he was overconfident. When it became obvious the game wasn't that easy, he got mad. He underestimated the game. Like—" He paused. He ran his hand through his hair and pushed it to one side. "Instead, be cautious. Don't be reckless, or else the Dark Wizard will overpower you. That's how he likes it. That's how he gains the upper hand."

Frustration swept through Ethan's body. Drake's habit of starting a sentence and not finishing it, along with his mysterious talk, told them nothing about the game. Drake knew something they did not. Ethan was sure of it. It could be something important. He felt the heat rise in him.

Ethan exchanged glances with his friends. If Drake knew something necessary, Ethan wanted to know what it was. "Wait a minute. You were about to say something and then you stopped."

Drake shifted his weight.

"Did you think we wouldn't notice?" Ethan's cheeks flushed.

"That's not important," Drake said and strode toward the end of the hall where Room Two was.

Anger bubbled up and Ethan clenched his fists. Drake was toying with them, which didn't help Ethan's mood. They wouldn't be able to play the game if Drake hid everything from them. He had to find out what Drake was about to say.

"Wait. Stop." Ethan followed Drake. He caught up with Drake outside the room. "You were talking about someone. Who?"

Drake fidgeted with his fingernails as Brody, Jason, and Alyssa rushed over. Drake shook his head. "I said too much already."

Ethan clenched his fists again. "Stop messing with us."

"Yo, man, calm down." Brody patted a hand on Ethan's back.

"Calm down?" He glanced at everyone, who all had a nervous

look on their face. Alyssa chewed her lip.

Drake sighed. "All I can tell you is you need to watch how you play the game. And whatever you do, avoid making deals. You *will* regret it." Drake shook his head. "Everyone does." With that, he led Team Dynamite to Room Two and motioned toward the door. "I believe this is where you begin today."

Drake's quick change of subject was not lost on Ethan, but he decided to let it go for now. He looked up and saw a sign on the wall next to the door that read in large brown letters "The Billiard Room."

Jason opened the door and went in first. Ethan followed. The room, which was much larger than the library, had chestnut brown walls. Picture frames hung in a line around the center of the room. The pictures inside all appeared to be of children. Golden pool sticks sat attached to racks.

In the middle of the room, a professional-sized mahogany pool table rested on a red Persian rug. The pool balls were racked up in the plastic triangle rack at the center of the table, waiting for the next game. Sitting next to the rack was a folded piece of white paper.

Ethan picked it up and read, "'Help us stop the gnome. Gordy the gnome is stealing our golden pool sticks. Stop him before he disappears with all of them. But beware, Gordy has many tricks of his own.'"

"This shouldn't be too hard," Alyssa said, walking over to the pool table. "It looks like we are already ahead. The pool sticks are still here."

No sooner had those words left Alyssa's mouth than a rumble came from under the pool table. The rug wiggled in a ripple pattern until it was pushed aside. A latch in the floor opened up with a pillar of smoke.

Ethan coughed and waved the smoke away from his face. When the rest of the smoke cleared, a tiny figure about two and a half feet tall rushed across the floor with intense speed. He had long, silvery hair with a few locks dangling over his forehead and into his eyes. He wore raggedy forest-green clothes and carried a little black sack over his shoulder. He turned to face the group and raised his big, bushy eyebrows as he teasingly reached out to touch a golden pool stick. His long round nose twitched before he snatched the first stick.

"Oh, no you don't," Brody called. He raced to tackle the gnome, but Gordy was too quick. He grabbed the stick and raced for the next one in the room.

"Does anyone know anything about gnomes?" Ethan called desperately. As he said that, he saw Alyssa in a corner staring at—no, reading a book. He rushed over to her. "Not now!" Ethan called as Gordy grabbed another stick. Brody chased after him, but Gordy snapped his fingers. With that, the rug rolled up and came tumbling after Brody.

Alyssa shook her head at Ethan. "It's not what you think. This wall here"—she smacked the wall with four firm hits—"is a secret door to the library."

As she said this, the sight of Jason rushing to help Brody caught Ethan's attention. Gordy had grabbed another pool stick. As the boys advanced, Gordy threw his hand forward and snapped his fingers. Both Brody and Jason flew backwards and landed on their backs.

Brody sat up and stared in amazement. "He's like a magician."

Jason rubbed his back. "A super strong one maybe."

Ethan turned his attention back to Alyssa. "Do you think you can find something quickly about this thing?"

"I'm already on it." She pointed to a pile of books on the floor on the other side of the wall-door. When she did that, one of her rings glistened in the light.

"Guys." Brody stood and dusted himself off. "Gordy only needs one more. What are we going to do?"

"Got it," Ethan called back. He raced to cut off the gnome before he reached the last pool stick, but the gnome had stopped. In fact, it seemed like the whole world stopped. Ethan followed Gordy's stare, which rested on Alyssa's ringed finger. "Alyssa, watch out!"

The gnome slowly strode toward her, his eyes fixated on her ring as Alyssa fumbled to take it off. The gnome leaped for Alyssa just as she threw it at Ethan. The gnome stopped and turned toward Ethan with an evil grin on his face.

"Uh, thanks, Alyssa."

"I'm sorry. I panicked."

Ethan ran with the ring. He made it halfway across the room before Gordy zipped in front of him. "Think, Ethan. Think," Ethan said out loud.

He glanced behind Gordy and saw that the hatch on the floor was still open.

"I have an idea," he called. "Follow my lead."

He lifted his chin to Jason and pointed his eyes toward the hatch in the floor. Jason nodded and stood on the other side of the hatch.

"Is this what you want, Gordy?" Ethan held the ring in between two fingers out in front of him.

Alyssa's eyes widened. "Don't. You. Dare!"

Ethan looked back at Gordy who was ready to charge at him. "It's the only way, Alyssa." She relaxed and nodded slowly.

Oh, I really hope Alyssa's ring isn't a real gem. Then again, this is only a game, right?

With that realization, he threw the ring down the open hatch.

Gordy tried to jump in after it, but the golden pool sticks in his hands blocked him. Alyssa ran toward the hatch, but Ethan stopped her. There was no way he was going to let her get trapped down there with the gnome. After struggling and straining, Gordy threw the golden pool sticks aside and chased after the ring. Instantly, Jason slammed the hatch closed. Brody grabbed a pool stick and levied it through the handle. Gordy pounded the hatch for several minutes before everything went silent. Ethan's heart thumped in his chest.

"Okay," Brody said, "that was intense."

Everyone nodded in agreement. Then a message blinked on the far wall. "Congratulations. You have survived Room Two!" Then the door slid open and they returned to the Great Hall. They saved their progress in the chamber and agreed to meet back on later that night. Ethan was beginning to get used to the prickly feeling after saving the game.

When Ethan exited the game and took his Transport off, the clock in front of him read 9:55 PM. He rubbed the back of his neck but froze when his eyes met his mom's angry eyes seconds later. She said nothing but pointed upstairs with a scowl on her face. He quickly obliged.

Guys, Ethan sent out in a group text. *Can't meet up later. It's 2 late and my mom is ticked...actually, livid is a better word.* He hated sending bad news to his friends.

Ethan thought things couldn't get any worse, but a few minutes later, Alyssa responded. "Well, if you think that's bad . . ." A picture came through following her last text. It was an image of Alyssa's hand. She was missing her ring.

CHAPTER 7 - Alyssa's Ring

"There's no way," Ethan said, pulling a book out of his locker at school the next day. "I thought you were kidding last night." He slammed his locker shut. But when he looked at Alyssa, the glare on her face made it clear she was not kidding.

"My. Ring. Is. Gone!" She held up her hand and flipped it back and forth to illustrate it was nowhere on her hand.

Guilt immediately crept through Ethan. If he thought for one minute they'd really lose her ring, he never would have thrown it to Gordy. He looked at Alyssa who looked like she was barely holding it together. He hated seeing her so upset.

"You know, this makes no sense," Brody said, coming to Ethan's defense. "Maybe you lost it after the game."

Jason nodded. "They're right. Think about what you're suggesting."

Alyssa's face turned beet red. "I know what I saw. I had the ring on when I started the game. Then *you*"—she pointed an accusing finger at Ethan—"threw it down a hole."

Ethan sucked in a breath. That really cut deep. He never intended to hurt Alyssa. All he was trying to do was get Team Dynamite away from the gnome. He sighed. It had to be somewhere. What happened in the game wasn't real . . . right?

He opened his mouth to suggest the idea, but she spoke first. "My grandmother gave it to me before she died last year." She frowned at her hand, staring at the empty space on her finger. "I wouldn't lose it."

"I don't understand, Alyssa. It's not like I *actually* threw your ring. That was in the game."

Alyssa trembled. "I know. But after we left the game—after you threw it down the hatch—my ring was gone." She looked around at everyone, her eyes begging them to believe her. "I don't know how it's possible either." She took a deep breath. "All I know is that it's true. Please! I need you to believe me."

Ethan felt another twinge of guilt. If he really was responsible for Alyssa losing her special ring, then he would be sure to find it. He hung his head and pulled her into a hug. The first thing he could do was go into the game and see if it was there. "I'm sorry. If that's what really happened, then we'll—no, *I'll* get it back."

Alyssa hugged him back. "Thank you," she whispered. He couldn't decide if she was thanking him for believing her or for vowing to get it back—or both.

At Study Hall, Ethan noticed Max still hadn't returned. He made a mental note to track down Max's girlfriend, Allie. Maybe she knew something. At lunch, Ethan went up to Allie's table, munching a few french fries at a time. "Hey, Allie, do you know what's going on with Max?"

"I have no idea." Allie shook her head. Her mousy brown ponytail bounced behind her. She pointed to Max's empty seat. "Max isn't here now, and he hasn't texted me back." She held her phone out to show him. "In fact, I haven't heard from him since a few days ago." She frowned. "Why would he disappear on me?"

Ethan shook his head. That wasn't like Max. He adored Allie. "I don't think it's just you. He hasn't been in any of my classes. Heck, I haven't even seen him on Seeker."

"Seeker," Allie echoed.

"Yea, I usually catch a glimpse of him in the Great Hall, but come to think of it, I haven't even seen him around there."

"That's . . . strange." Allie's voice almost sounded far away. "The last time we talked, he said something about a challenge associated with Seeker."

"That is strange," Ethan said. "Have you stopped by his house? Maybe he's sick."

"No. I thought he was avoiding me, so I wanted to give him space. But maybe I will stop by, if only to assure myself that he is okay." Allie's forehead wrinkled with worry, but she recovered. "I'm sure we'll figure it out. It probably really is nothing."

"Yeah, I'm sure you're right. When I go on tonight, I'll look for him."

As soon as Ethan got home, he threw his school bag on the table and rushed over to the gaming console. Maggie rushed upstairs to her room as Ethan began setting up the game. Maggie returned a few minutes later with a large yellow poster board.

"What's that?" Ethan asked. He adjusted the Transport headset and tested the mic.

Maggie flipped the poster board around. Ethan looked up, and the sign read:

Monday – four hours

Tuesday – six hours

"How long will it be today?" Maggie demanded, tapping her foot.

"Not lo—"

"Don't say 'not long.' You *always* say that. Do you know I cooked dinner last night? Alone. I ate dinner by myself."

Ethan tilted his head to one side. "I'm pretty sure Mom was home for that."

Maggie shook her head. "She was later than she thought she'd be . . . but you would know that if you got off that game." She pointed her head toward the kitchen. "Did you even stop to eat? And why do I have to start sounding like Mom now?" Maggie was so worked up that she had to stop to catch her breath.

"Okay, okay. I'll get off earlier and we'll watch a movie together."

Maggie gave him a doubtful look, but she relaxed. "We'll see." She walked away with the sign but paused, turned, and said, "FYI, Mom has become *obsessed* with your grades, so if you are missing anything, you may want to fix that." With that, she disappeared upstairs.

He took a deep breath and started Seeker. He knew he should probably play later and hang out with Maggie, but he would catch up with her after the game, like they agreed.

When he arrived in Seeker, Ethan scanned the other players gathering in the Great Hall. There were even more people than last time. *Lots* more. But the one person he didn't see was Max. When the rest of Team Dynamite arrived, Ethan explained his conversation with Allie and how he said he'd see if Max was around.

"I don't see him," Brody said after a while.

Jason nodded. "Me neither."

"Same," Alyssa said with a frown. "And don't let me see that gnome. If I do, he's going to wish he never met me."

"Wow," Jason said. "Never mess with Alyssa and her jewelry."

"What's this about jewelry?" Drake appeared behind the group.

Ethan jumped. He wished Drake wouldn't sneak up on them like that.

Alyssa spun on him. "Your gnome *stole* my ring!" She glared at him. "Why?"

Ethan folded his arms. *This ought to be good.*

Drake held both hands in the air in front of him. "Hey, he's not my gnome. And if I know anything about Nith and Seeker, at best, the ring was used to ensure your return." He gave Alyssa a pointed look. "And here you are." He turned to Ethan. "Though I must admit, that was the most creative way I've seen that room defeated yet."

Ethan felt his eyes narrow as Alyssa looked like she was about to explode.

Drake cleared his throat. "Let us move on to Room Three." He led the group down the length of the hall.

"Not without my—" Alyssa started.

Drake cut her off. "We'll keep our eyes open for it, okay?"

Alyssa looked doubtful, but they continued. As they walked, they passed the section of the hallway where the Shadow Room was that Ethan had noticed the other day. Once again, he thought a shadow zipped past the window. He stopped and peeked through the window. At first, there was nothing, but as his eyes adjusted to the dark, the tables he saw last time became clearer. They sat arranged in neat symmetrical rows and on top of the tables were lines of computers evenly spaced out and lined up directly in front of each other. Keyboards sat centered in front of the computer monitors. A computer mouse rested on the right side of the keyboards, each glowing slightly red underneath. He was about to turn back to the group when he spotted a figure staring right back at him. The creature's eyes widened, then he turned around and dashed deeper into the room.

"Guys," Ethan called. "I see something." Something about the creature was familiar, but it was so dark that Ethan couldn't put his finger on it. Maybe that's why he wasn't as freaked out about this creature as he was before. The only familiar thing he could think of was how fast it was. Then it dawned on him. The only speedy thing he'd met so far in Seeker was Gordy. Everyone ran over and joined Ethan outside the Shadow Room. "There's something in there," he said. "He's a fast, little creature."

Brody stepped forward and peered through the window. "Do you think it's another gnome?"

Alyssa pushed to the front of the group. "Maybe it knows something about my ring." She grabbed the doorknob. "I'm going to find out!"

Ethan jumped in front of her. He wasn't going to make her do this on her own.

"Only if we go with you." Ethan looked at everyone for their agreement. Everyone nodded.

Drake had a slight smile on his face. Ethan couldn't figure out why he was smiling, but it wasn't the time for that. "Remember," Drake said, "he can hear you. When he wants to, he can also see you. And *never* accept a challenge or make a deal."

Honestly, Drake can be so dramatic, Ethan thought, but he reflected on one word: challenge. *Didn't Allie say something about Max and a challenge?*

Drake stepped forward. "You won't be able to get in without my access." He stepped in front of Alyssa and held out his

Guardian of Bailiwick chain that he always wore around his neck. A beep emerged from the door and the lock clicked. Drake held out his arm. "After you."

Alyssa opened the door and Ethan and the rest of Team Dynamite set out to hunt down the creature. They split up throughout the room as they checked under the tables and around the computers. Ethan turned on the flashlight feature of his Transport and then took a quick glance around the room. A small wooden desk hid in the shadows of the corner. As he made his way over to it, something glistened under the desk. Ethan ran toward it, and the creature scurried out from underneath. *Was that actually Gordy? I know it has to be a gnome, but what are the chances?* The creature dashed across the room. His long silver hair trailed behind him as he raced toward the computer tables at lightning speed. *Yep, that's Gordy. But isn't he part of the billiard room level?* Ethan shook his head. So. Many. Questions. "Focus, Ethan," he whispered to himself.

"Gordy, stop," Ethan called. Instead of stopping, Gordy jumped on top of the tables, knocking over some of the computer monitors and displacing the keyboards.

Ethan darted to the front and center of the room where the first table sat. Gordy finally paused. He held up Alyssa's ring tauntingly and smiled. Alyssa, Brody, and Jason quickly ran to the other side of the table.

So many questions raced through Ethan's mind as he and his friends exchanged glances. *Is that really her ring? How was he able to keep it after Alyssa left the game? And most importantly, shouldn't he be in the billiard room waiting for the next gamers?*

Alyssa scowled. "Give me my ring back," she commanded.

Gordy shook his head. "I got it fair and square," he said in a shaky, squeaky voice. He snapped his fingers and the lights in the room came on. "Although . . ." He paused as he rolled the ring between his fingers and flashed a slimy smile. "I'm always up for cutting a deal."

CHAPTER 8 - The Race

Everything in Ethan screamed, "Don't do it." Even Drake's voice echoed in his head: "Never make a deal, never make a deal, never make a deal." But when he looked over at Alyssa, she looked like she was going to cry. He turned and looked at Jason and Brody, who both shook their heads emphatically. But he had promised her he would get it back. He had to do it. He was *going* to do it.

"I don't have a good feeling about this," Jason said.

Neither did Ethan, but his mind was made up. "What kind of deal?" Ethan blurted out.

Alyssa's jaw dropped and she shook her head. "I can't let you do that."

Ethan looked at her. "I gave it to him, so I'll make it right by getting it back." He then turned to Gordy. "What kind of deal?"

Gordy's smile widened. He snapped his fingers and the ring disappeared.

"You little—" Alyssa growled, but Gordy cut her off.

"I've hidden the ring in this room. If you can find it, you can keep it."

Ethan breathed a sigh of relief. That didn't sound too hard.

"What's the catch?" Brody folded his arms and stared at the gnome.

"Ahh, yes," Gordy agreed. "There has to be something in it for me." His wide eyes roamed around the room as he made eye contact with everyone there. "You will have ten minutes to find the ring. If you find it before time runs out, you keep the ring. *But*, if you don't, I keep the ring and you remain in Seeker forever."

"That is ludicrous," Jason seethed. "You are aware that we can leave at any time, right? It's a *game*."

Brody nudged him.

"That is only because *he* allows you to leave." Gordy folded his arms.

Something in Ethan snapped. He threw his hands up in the air and closed in on Gordy. Ethan was tired of hearing about this "he" character that Drake always talked about, and now Gordy. "Who is *he*?" Ethan demanded.

"Oh, I'm sure you'll meet the Dark Wizard soon enough." Gordy waved a hand dismissively. "Now, do we have a deal?"

Ethan held up his hand. "Woah. One second. What do you mean 'remain in Seeker forever,' and while we're at it, just who is this Dark Wizard?"

Gordy smirked at him. "No more questions. Do we have a deal or not?"

Again, everything in him screamed, "Don't do it." But he had to fix it. "You guys don't have to do this with me," Ethan said, and then he turned back to Gordy. "But I owe this to Alyssa."

"No." Alyssa grabbed Ethan's arm. "It's not that important. This deal seems . . . final."

Ethan surprised even himself when he said, "I've already decided. I'm doing this."

"Well, I'm not letting you do this alone," Brody said and stood next to Ethan. "If you're in, I'm in."

"Me too," Jason said and walked up to the other side of Ethan.

Alyssa let go of Ethan's arm. "You're all crazy, you know that?" She looked at them and then said, "Well, it's *my* ring. I can't let you guys do this while I do nothing."

Ethan grinned at his friends. "Let's do this."

"Let's do this," they answered.

"Well, then." Gordy rubbed his hands together. "It's settled." He snapped his fingers again and a digital clock set at ten minutes hung in the air. "Your time starts now. Ten minutes."

Everyone immediately split up in four different directions. They each took a corner of the room. They searched under the tables, lifted keyboards, and slid computers aside, but they found nothing. Ethan scanned the walls to see if there were any small nooks that the ring might be hidden in, but the walls were all smooth.

Gordy sat back and examined his fingers as everyone scurried around.

Ethan glanced at the digital clock in the air: 7:18.

When Ethan checked with his friends, they all had similar luck. "Maybe it's near the desk," Ethan said. "That's where he was hiding when we first got in here."

Alyssa ripped out all the drawers to the desk and dumped them on the floor. She swam through papers, but no ring. No matter where they searched on the desk, there was no ring.

"I don't even think he hid the ring," Jason said.

Alyssa nodded. "I'm starting to think the same thing."

Ethan sighed and checked the clock again: 3:52.

Where could it be? The computers had nothing. The walls had nothing. Even the desk had nothing. The desk.

Remembering the way the flashlight beams reflected off the ring earlier, he wondered if he could find it again. He hoped so. He knew he had to act quickly. He ran over to the entrance of the room and flipped the switch.

"Ethan, what are you doing?" Alyssa cried. "How are we supposed to see?"

"I got ya." Brody pointed at Ethan. He reached for the top of his headset and pressed a button, activating the flashlight. "Everyone do the same."

Ethan ran past the clock: 2:17.

The group frantically scanned every inch of the room with their flashlights. Nothing.

Alyssa gasped and pointed at the tables. "Over there."

Gordy scrambled to his feet. Ethan caught a glimpse of him out of the corner of his eye. Did Gordy seem anxious?

The clock kept ticking away: 1:06.

Everyone rushed over to the center table that Alyssa pointed to.

"Fifty-five seconds," Jason called out.

The gnome paced back and forth.

Ethan's eyes narrowed. "You must be on to something, Alyssa. Just look at Gordy."

Gordy continued pacing and wringing his wrists. When Ethan looked closer at the computer Alyssa pointed out, the computer had a different mouse. All the other mice in the room had red lasers under it, but the middle computer of the center table had a mouse with a blue-tinted light. Ethan shoved the keyboard out of the way and lifted up the mouse. Right in the center where the mouse's laser light should have been was Alyssa's ring. Ethan snatched it up just as the clock hit zero.

"AAARGHHH," Gordy shrieked. "This is not over! The Dark

Wizard will not be pleased with me. It's bad enough you got past me in the billiard room." He chewed his green, gnomey fingernails. Ethan handed Alyssa her ring. She slipped it back on her finger, glaring at Gordy. Then, with a nod and a snap of his fingers, Gordy vanished.

Alyssa reached over and pulled Ethan into a hug. "Thank you," she whispered. His heart warmed. He didn't know if it was the release of guilt off his shoulders or a response to yet another weird escape from Seeker, but her hug made him feel better. Things were right again.

He finally let go when he caught Jason nudging Brody and pointing at them. Alyssa and Ethan quickly moved away from each other. Ethan cleared his throat. "Let's get out of here."

As Team Dynamite exited the room, Ethan's legs felt like jelly. Drake greeted them with a solemn look. "I warned you not to make any deals."

"I know," Ethan answered. "And we wouldn't have, but Alyssa's ring . . ."

Drake nodded. "I understand, but you have no idea how much you risked today."

"Yeah, about that." Brody stepped forward. "Who is this Dark Wizard Gordy keeps referring to?"

If computerized people could turn pale, that is exactly what Drake did. "You need to go." When everyone stared at him, he added, "NOW!" Then he ushered them off to the chamber down the hall and closed the door. Ethan pressed *Save* and the familiar prickly feeling told him the save was successful.

CHAPTER 9 - Lord Nith

Ethan woke up in the morning on his living room floor, clutching his controller and headset. He didn't remember falling asleep, but he was wide awake when his mom came downstairs.

"I don't believe this," his mom yelled. "Were you on the game *all night?*"

Ethan jumped to his feet. "Well . . . ugh . . . not all night." At least he thought that was true. He stretched and rubbed his eyes.

"We will discuss this later. For now, get ready for school."

As Ethan rushed up the stairs, he passed Maggie who was on her way down. She refused to look at him, and his heart sank. He completely forgot about the movie he promised her last night. As he rushed his way to his room, he vowed to make it up to her, but right now he had to get to school before his mom grounded him for a month. Minutes later, he grabbed his school bag and ran out the door.

At lunchtime, Ethan met up with his friends at their table. When everyone was settled, Brody asked the group, "Anyone else getting completely creeped out by Seeker?"

"A little," Ethan agreed. "But it is—"

"Just a game," everyone finished for him.

"I feel really bad though," Ethan said as he took a sip of his milkshake. "I was supposed to spend some time with Maggie. I promised her, and then before I knew it, I was on all night."

Brody frowned. "Aww, man, I know she was looking forward to it."

Ethan nodded.

"What about Max?" Jason asked and popped two french fries in his mouth at the same time. "Has anyone heard any updates on him?"

Everyone shook their heads. Ethan had scanned the crowds when he and his friends were in Seeker the night before, but he never saw him. Worse, Max still hadn't returned to school and there were rumors that he had disappeared. Allie looked like she hadn't slept in days. It wasn't until just before dismissal that more news arrived. Principal Jones addressed it over afternoon announcements.

After announcing all the club meetings for the day, his voice turned serious. "I have some disturbing news." He cleared his throat and continued. "Max Vesper's parents have filed a missing person's report. He has been missing since the beginning of the week." Principal Jones paused, allowing time for students to gasp from the shock. "He was last seen walking home on Monday. The police are working around the clock to find him. In the meantime, I urge all of you to use caution going to and from school. Stay in groups, and above all, avoid detours." As the announcement ended, there was a deafening silence in the classroom.

Ethan couldn't shake the uneasy feeling churning inside. Ethan had only seen Max in the game that Monday. Sure, it was a few days ago, but to be labeled as missing so soon?

"Well, maybe someone logged in as him," Brody reasoned as

they walked home from school. "And that's why you saw him on there." He stopped and a look of realization brushed across his face. "Maybe it was Allie trying to contact Max's friends to see what they knew."

Jason held up his phone. "Wouldn't this be easier?"

Alyssa shook her head. "Not if she doesn't know their numbers. Think about it." She put her hands in her hoodie's pockets. "Everyone's playing Seeker now. What could be faster to reach all his friends than contacting them all at once?"

Ethan wasn't convinced, but it didn't matter. Max was gone, and he shouldn't be.

A few minutes later, everyone headed to their houses. Ethan still had a few blocks to go. His thoughts wandered back to Maggie as he got closer to home. A guilty feeling emerged as he thought about how disappointed she was yesterday when he never got off his game. He seemed to be disappointing a lot of people lately. All Maggie really wanted was to spend some time with him. *Well,* Ethan decided, *I'm going to fix that today.* Learning about Max's disappearance made him realize how quickly things could change. All he had to do was think about his dad disappearing to prove that point. He shouldn't have let his sister down. He had to do better, no matter how much Seeker tempted him.

"Maggie," Ethan called as he walked in the door. He froze when he entered the living room. Maggie had the Transport in her hands, ready to put it on. "Maggie, stop. What are you doing?" When he finally was able to make his legs work, he rushed over to her.

"I want to see what the big deal is." She lifted the Transport over her head and slid on the headset. "Everyone is playing it and talking about it at school." Her eyes shifted to the TV.

"And you're obsessed with it, so it must be good."

Ethan grabbed the headset off her head. The thought of Maggie playing the game frightened him. "You can't," he said. "Something isn't right about this game."

Maggie rolled her eyes and reached for the headset again. "It's because you don't want me to play."

Ethan was too quick for her and swiped the headset out of her reach. "That's not it. I can't explain it, but even Brody is getting creeped out by it."

Maggie paused for a minute. Brody was the most levelheaded of all Ethan's friends. Because of that, he was the one people went to for advice. Especially Maggie.

"So, does that mean you are done playing it?"

Ethan looked away. The hope in her eyes brightened her face, and he didn't have the heart to tell her he planned to continue playing until he figured out what was going on. He had decided not to play too much and spend more time with his sister, but he also had to find out what was going on.

"That's what I thought." The hope vanished from her eyes. She pushed past him and rushed upstairs.

This was so not the way Ethan planned their conversation. He followed her upstairs to her room, but it was already locked shut.

"Go away," she said when he knocked.

Buzzz! Ethan's phone interrupted him. He pulled it out and opened the message. Jason had texted the group. *You guys up for another game of Seeker?* Ethan looked at Maggie's door, trying to decide what to do. He knocked again lightly on her door.

Something thumped against the door. "I said go away!"

Ethan's phone lit up with messages about meeting on Seeker.

He sighed and left Maggie alone as she asked.

Within minutes, Team Dynamite was gathered in the Great Hall. Usually, Drake was there to meet them, but he was nowhere to be found. "I'm not going anywhere until he shows up," Ethan said. "He was acting strange the last time we were together."

Everyone gave him a look that said *come on.*

"I mean stranger than usual," Ethan clarified.

"Normal is boring," Drake said, interrupting the group as he appeared against the wall across from them. His arms were folded and his left foot was pressed up against the bottom of the wall.

Once again, Ethan jumped. "Seriously. Stop doing that."

Drake grinned.

As frustrated as Ethan was with Drake's games, he couldn't help but feel a moment of relief. He had a feeling Drake knew more than he was letting on, and they needed him for that information. And they *would* get it from him.

Ethan shifted his weight. "So, what was that all about yesterday? You practically kicked us all out of the game."

Drake pushed himself off the wall and moved closer to Ethan. He stared directly into Ethan's eyes, which made Ethan squirm. Drake backed up. Ethan let out a breath he didn't know he was holding. "You changed the game," Drake said, his tone serious.

Everyone began shouting at once.

"What?"

"How?"

"What are you talking about?"

Drake held up a hand to silence everyone. "When you accepted the deal with the gnome—and won—you got the attention of Lord Nith."

"How are we supposed to know what that means?" Alyssa asked.

Drake nodded toward the Shadow Room. "Gordy refers to Nith as the Dark Wizard."

Jason, Brody, and Ethan all exchanged a look.

"So, we got the attention of another game character," Ethan said, trying to push all the nagging thoughts out of his head that were telling him they were in way over their heads.

Drake shook his head. "This is Lord Nith's world. And right now, all of you are a threat to it."

As if on cue, a black swirling cloud appeared by the Grand Stairway. All the other players that were buzzing around the Grand Hall vanished. Sparks of purple lightning surrounded the cloud. The cloud evaporated as a tall, thin figure emerged. He wore a black cloak that brushed the floor. He pushed the hood off his head. Lord Nith's long, black hair reached the middle of his back and his beard was just as long. He held a staff as tall as he was that was made of wood and intertwined with gold. A glowing ball of light purple energy rested on top. He turned and looked straight at Ethan. His narrow slit-shaped eyes held a stare that felt like it could pierce Ethan's soul.

CHAPTER 10 - Missing

Nith eyed the group up and down. "These are the people who defeated Gordy," he sneered, then threw his head back with a laugh. "Don't worry. He won't be making those mistakes again."

"He. Stole. My. Ring," Alyssa said, gritting her teeth.

Nith turned and stared at her, and Alyssa immediately shrunk back. He cracked an evil smile, circling the group. He stopped in front of Ethan as he examined his staff. He looked up and stared Ethan in the eyes. "How's your friend Max doing these days?"

Ethan's heart skipped a beat. How did Nith know about Max? Unless . . .

"Yes," Nith said as if reading Ethan's mind.

Brody, Jason, and Alyssa moved in closer to Ethan.

"Max loves Seeker. In fact"—Nith caressed the top of the staff—"he practically lives here."

Jason rushed up to Nith, leaving only inches between them.

Drake straightened. "I wouldn't do that."

But it was too late. Nith lowered his staff and aimed. A purple light zipped from the staff right at Jason's feet. Jason jumped back just in time. A smoking singed oval emerged where Jason once stood.

Ethan gulped. "What do you know about Max?" He knew this was impossible, yet here he was having a conversation with a video game villain about his missing friend.

Nith waved the staff and an image projected onto the wall that showed a dark, windowless room. It was hard for Ethan to make anything out, but as the projection panned around the room, a figure sat slumped against the wall holding his knees to this chest.

"Is th-that—" Alyssa whispered, but she couldn't finish the sentence.

"Max." Jason glared at Nith.

"Max," Brody called and ran closer to the projection. "Max, it's us."

Nith laughed and shut off the image. "He can't hear you. That was a projection—a video, if you will—of my dungeons."

"So you're telling us that you have Max?" Jason clarified. "Why?"

Nith shrugged. "He lost. He made a deal and lost." Nith clicked his tongue. "What people will trade for an extra game life. And now, it's your turn." Nith lifted his staff in the air.

"Run," Drake yelled.

"But we won the deal with Gord—" Alyssa protested.

Drake pointed to the chamber. "Go! Now."

Ethan hesitated, then dashed down the hall. Brody and Jason were behind him. Alyssa still seemed frozen. Ethan ran back for her. He reached for her hand and pulled her to him. "We'll figure it out later," he whispered. "Let's go." She smiled at him and gave his hand a squeeze. Then they sped off with their friends.

They ran back down the Great Hall and over to the chamber. Purple lightning bolts nipped at their feet as they made their way. As they rushed off, he thought of Max. What would Nith be doing to him?

"Wait," Ethan said. "We can't leave Max here."

More lightning bolts whizzed by them, missing their heads by inches.

Brody shook his head. "Not now. We need a plan."

Jason nodded in agreement.

The group burst through the chamber and slid the door closed. Ethan caught a quick glimpse of Drake, who had a mix of fear and sorrow on his face.

"We'll be back," Ethan promised. He pressed the save button and exited the game, bringing himself back to his own living room. He stood there, staring at the TV, only half believing what he witnessed. His hands were shaking, and he took deep breaths to calm his racing heart.

He turned his head and a glare from his mom greeted him. He groaned.

"Two words: you're grounded."

"Wh-why?" Ethan threw his hands in the air.

"Do you have *any* idea what time it is?" Mom pointed to the watch on her wrist. "One A.M!"

No way. She had to be wrong.

"You missed dinner. You kept saying you were on your way. Then I sent you to bed hours ago. And now I woke up to you screaming at that thing." She pointed to the console.

Ethan definitely didn't remember that.

"It's like this game is turning you into a zombie." She looked at Ethan and her face softened a little bit. "No games tomorrow—well, today."

Ethan nodded and then stopped. "Wait. I can't. I prom—"

Mom held out her hand. "Non-negotiable. No games today."

"But this is imp—"

"I *said* it is non-negotiable."

"You don't understand. Something's going on. I have to—"

Mom pointed up the stairs. "I said no." She picked up the controller and held it. "And to be sure, I'm taking this."

"Ugh. That's not fair."

Mom shrugged. "Now, get to bed."

"This sucks. Why are you so mean? Nobody else has to deal with this." He stormed up the steps and slammed his door. He thought he caught a glimpse of hurt in her eyes, but he was too frustrated to think about it. He couldn't believe she was doing this. He had to get to the game and find out what had happened to Max and how to get him out of there. Nobody could help him but Ethan and his friends, especially since nobody would believe Max was kidnapped by a video game. She didn't understand. He took a few deep breaths and tried to relax. He *would* find a way to get back on Seeker.

Ethan finally fell asleep, catching the few hours of sleep he had left, dreaming of a way to get back on Seeker in time to help Max.

* * *

"If I have to call your name one more time, I'm throwing you in the shower." Ethan's mom towered over him as he struggled to open his eyes. "Get up. Now."

"Okay, okay," he grumbled. That was so annoying. Her voice was *not* the first one he wanted to hear that morning. He took a deep breath and tried to change his mood. He didn't need more trouble. It was hard though. Every time he thought about the game, it brought twinges of the frustration he felt last night.

When he came downstairs, Maggie was finishing breakfast at the kitchen table.

"Hey, Maggs." Ethan threw an arm around her shoulder.

Maggie shrugged it off, got up, and walked away.

"Still mad at me, I see." He tucked his head down and gave her an overdramatic frown.

Maggie glared at him and walked out the door.

"Ouch," Brody said as he walked past Maggie and into the house. "She's still not talking to you, huh?"

Ethan shook his head as his mom gave him a stern look.

"Let's go," Brody said and pushed Ethan to the door. "The tension in here is thicker than peanut butter."

As they walked to school, they met up with Jason and Alyssa.

"What's wrong?" Alyssa asked Ethan. "You look terrible."

Alyssa was probably right. He was wearing the same blue T-shirt and jeans from yesterday, and he hadn't had time that morning to even smooth over his curls. He was surprised his mom hadn't said anything before he left, though she probably expected it since he was up so late. But none of this was what was bothering him.

"Maggie won't talk to me," Ethan said. "I try to apologize to her when I see her, but she doesn't even look at me."

"She didn't tell you before what was bugging her?" Alyssa asked as the group stepped off a curb to cross the street.

"Well, yeah, sort of."

"And?"

"He spends too much time on Seeker," Brody answered for Ethan.

Ethan gave him a look but was grateful he didn't have to say it out loud himself.

"Yeah," Jason added.

"Weren't you supposed to watch a movie with her one night?"

Ethan sighed. "I know. It's not like I meant to ignore her."

"Maybe you should plan a special day with her," Alyssa suggested. "Take her shopping, or to the movies, or to get her hair done."

Ethan smiled. He knew Maggie would love it, but he would probably have to convince her to talk to him first. He wouldn't blame her if she refused. He had broken promises to her before. As much as he deserved it, Ethan hoped he could convince her to come out with him. As they approached the school building, Ethan promised himself that he would be there for Maggie this time.

School was strange. Everyone was talking about Max's disappearance. Policemen were patrolling the neighborhood at arrival and dismissal time. Everyone was whispering theories on what had happened to Max. Ethan shivered. He knew what had happened to Max. He wished he could shout it in the hallway, but saying something like, "Hey, I know where Max is. He's trapped in a video game by an evil wizard," would pretty much make everyone wonder about his sanity.

"Hey, we have to meet somewhere so we can figure out a plan," Ethan said as he passed Jason in the hall.

"Definitely," Jason answered. "The sooner the better."

Later that day, they all met at Alyssa's after school since she lived the closest. Jason, Brody, Ethan, and Alyssa all sat at her kitchen table, which was full of potato chips, sodas, and cookies.

"Who do we have over?" Alyssa's dad asked, eyeing each of the boys.

Alyssa rolled her eyes. "Daaaaad."

"Okay." He held his hands up. "But I'll be right here." He

pointed to the adjacent room. "In the next room." He slowly walked out, never taking his eyes off of the boys.

Alyssa blushed but quickly changed the subject. "How do you think we should do this?"

"I think the first thing to do is locate the dungeon," Brody said. "We could try to sneak Max out, but something tells me it won't be that easy."

For over an hour, everyone shot around ideas of what they thought they should or shouldn't do, and they were no closer to having a plan than before they started.

"It looks like the only plan we came up with so far is that we don't go back to the game without a plan," Alyssa said.

That worked for Ethan since he was grounded from the game anyway. When he left Alyssa's house, he practiced all the way home on how he would apologize to Maggie and tell her about his "Ethan and Maggie Day" he had planned. He just hoped she would hear him out. When he reached the house, he took a deep breath as he turned the doorknob.

"Maggie," he called as he entered the front door. He looked around but didn't see her. Maybe she was somewhere else in the house. "Maggie," he called again louder. No answer. "Maggs," he called again and went upstairs to check her room. No Maggie. *Maybe she went to her friend's house,* he thought.

He searched the rest of the rooms upstairs, just in case he missed her somehow, but found nothing. His heart sank. Now that he had a way to make up for not being around as much, he had to wait to tell her about it.

He headed back downstairs and sat on the living room couch. That's when he noticed that the TV was on. Not only that, but the "Welcome to Seeker" message lingered on the screen.

His heart caught in his throat. *She didn't try to play Seeker, did she? No. She couldn't have. Mom took the controller.* He moved closer. The game controller and Transport headset sat scattered on the floor in front of the TV.

Well, well, Ethan thought to himself, grinning, *it looks like Maggie found the controller.* Then his smile faded and his heart skipped a beat. He hoped he would not get in trouble for that. Would his mom even believe he had nothing to do with this? He turned his attention back to the gaming area. It looked as if the controller and headset had been dropped in a rush. Maggie would never do that, especially if she took the controller from their mom's hiding spot. If she was done playing, she would put everything away. But, if she was playing the game, why wasn't she there? In the room? Using the Transport and controller? That was when a thought occurred to Ethan. One that he didn't want to acknowledge. *Could it be that Maggie is trapped in the game? Like Max?* He hoped that ridiculous thought was wrong, but if he was right, Maggie would be the second person in their neighborhood who vanished in the game.

I can't find Maggie, he texted Brody, Alyssa, and Jason. *Then I found this...* Ethan sent a photo of the gaming area by the TV showing that it was all set up but nobody was there. His stomach turned at giving a voice to the terrifying thought in his head. *I think she's in the game,* he added. *Like, actually inside the game. I can't think of any other explanation.*

He wasn't sure it was even possible, yet a feeling inside him already knew. Maggie was trapped. And Ethan had no idea how to get her out.

CHAPTER 11 - Missing

Within minutes, Brody, Jason, and Alyssa joined Ethan in his living room. He had left the gaming area exactly how he found it. They all went back and forth trying to come up with a logical explanation.

"Maybe she went for a walk," Alyssa suggested. "Or maybe she's hanging out at her friend's place because she's still mad at you."

"Maybe she left the living room like that on purpose," Brody offered. "To get you in more trouble."

"Nah," Ethan responded. "She wouldn't do that."

"I wouldn't be too sure. She was *mad.* Like m-a-d—mad at you," Jason said.

"Why don't we go into Seeker?" Alyssa suggested. "Let's see if we can find her anywhere. That way we can rule this out." She looked at everyone. "My guess is she's over at a friend's house."

Ethan nodded. "It will make me feel better."

"Okay, give us fifteen minutes to get home and logged in," Alyssa said.

Fifteen minutes later, they gathered in Seeker's Great Hall by the Grand Stairway. Ethan shook as they waited for Drake to arrive. Drake often arrived immediately after they did. After several minutes, they decided to see if they could call him.

"Drake?" Jason called. Other players in the Grand Hall turned their way. When Drake didn't respond, Jason called again. Still nothing. Jason motioned for everyone else to call too.

"Drake." The word echoed with the sounds of everyone's voices. Silence followed the echoes.

"That's perfect." Jason threw his hands up in the air. "When we really need him, he's nowhere to be found."

"Shh!" Drake appeared behind Jason. "What part of 'he can hear you' don't you understand?"

Jason jumped from the shock of hearing Drake's voice.

Ethan gave Drake a death glare. "Stop doing that!" He threw his hands on his hips. "And maybe we wouldn't have to yell like that if you joined us the first time."

Jason let out a quick laugh.

Ethan cleared his throat. "Anyway. Sorry for yelling, Drake. We need your input right now, and you weren't here. We didn't know what else to do."

"It's bad, isn't it?" Drake's eyebrows wrinkled with concern.

Everyone nodded.

"I was trying to steer clear of you guys. I'm on Lord Nith's hit list right now since I helped you get out of here. And he's definitely not thrilled with your group."

"You told us the game changed last time we were here." Alyssa moved closer and stood next to Drake.

Drake nodded.

Alyssa glanced at Ethan and then continued. "Another person is missing."

Drake brought his hand up to his forehead, and Ethan knew that couldn't be good.

"It's starting," Drake whispered. He walked to the third door in the wall and rested his hand against it as if he were touching something on the other side. He dropped his hand and turned to the group. "I don't want to ask, for I fear the answer. Who is missing now?"

"Maggie. My sister, Maggie." Ethan's voice cracked. His eyes were downcast and he could barely look at anyone.

Drake nodded. "That's what I thought."

Brody pushed Ethan behind him. "What does that mean? We didn't even know if she was here."

Drake stepped to the side and locked eyes with Ethan. "He's using your sister to lure you into his trap. Let's find out where she is." Drake waved them along. "Follow me." He approached the grand stairs, but this time he climbed up. Ethan approached the stairs and peered behind them. It looked like there were more steps on the opposite side.

When Ethan hesitated, Drake motioned for him to follow. A large oval mirror hung on the wall at the top of the stairs. On both sides of the wall were marble bridges that led to pathways down the hall. Ethan looked over and saw that the stairs from the other side also led to the bridges.

He turned his attention back to the mirror on the wall. Alyssa looked in the mirror and tucked a few loose locks of hair behind her ponytail. As she stood there, her reflection began to ripple the way a tiny pebble would ripple water in a pond. She jumped back and her foot slipped down a step. Ethan, who was right next to her, saw her slip. He quickly reached out and grabbed her, pulling her closer to him. *Did she just blush?*

"Thanks." She smiled at him.

Drake cleared his throat loudly. "This is not any old mirror," Drake explained. "Lord Nith has several of these throughout the castle. It is one of his security measures." Then he turned to the mirror and said, "Show me the prisoners."

Ethan shivered at the word "prisoners."

The ripples in the mirror grew larger and larger, blurring the current reflections. When the ripples cleared, they were no longer staring at their own reflection. Instead, a dark room made of stone appeared. This was a larger room than the one from Lord Nith's projection the day before. The door was made of steel and there was only one small rectangular window at the top of the wall where a thin ray of light poured in. That wasn't the only difference. Instead of Max sitting by himself, a young, blonde-haired girl slept on the ground next to him. It was Maggie. Ethan's stomach soured. She was so still.

"Is that her?" Drake asked.

All Ethan could do was nod.

"Is she okay?" Brody managed to get the question out before Ethan could speak.

Drake nodded. "Neither of them are hurt. They're waiting."

"Waiting for what?" Ethan spun around to face Drake.

Drake winced and looked down at his shoes. It was the first time Ethan saw him so concerned. "Lord Nith will be using them—and any other prisoners—in his plan."

"What plan?" Alyssa, Jason, Brody, and Ethan asked in unison.

Drake shook his head and headed back down the grand stairs. "I have said too much."

Ethan could no longer hold his frustration back. His sister was stuck in Seeker with no way out, and Drake was concerned about saying too much.

"Oh, no you don't." Ethan raced down the stairs after him.

"This is my sister. If you know something, tell us."

Brody appeared next to Ethan. "I thought your role in this game was to help us, Drake. To guide us."

Alyssa and Jason followed close behind.

"This is no longer a game," Drake said, staring at the floor.

"But you'll still help us, right?" Ethan asked. After all, Drake had been holding out on them. If they had any chance of freeing Max and Maggie—or even surviving themselves—they'd need whatever information Drake had. However, Drake either didn't hear the statement or ignored it, because he gave no response.

"Dude, that's cold." Jason shook his head.

"Drake." Alyssa walked around the group and stood in front of him. "Look at me." Drake pulled his eyes from the floor and looked directly at Alyssa. "If this was your sister—your family—wouldn't you want every opportunity to help her?"

Drake seemed to struggle for several minutes. He paced back and forth. Stopped. Opened his mouth to speak. Then paced again. Finally, he stopped again. He whispered something to Alyssa and then went into the Shadow Room down toward the front of the hall.

Ethan, Brody, and Jason began to protest as Drake walked away. Alyssa held up her hand as if to shush everyone, but Ethan wasn't sure. Drake had been hiding so much. Now he wanted them to trust him? Would it even be possible?

Alyssa looked around and then whispered, "Drake said to meet him in the Shadow Room." She smiled for the first time that day. "He's going to help us."

Tears burned Ethan's eyes. He trusted Alyssa's judgment. If she was prepared to trust Drake, then he could too. At last, a shred of hope burned in him. Would he finally find out what was really going on and how to help his sister? He needed to fix this. All she ever wanted was to spend time with him, and now she was stuck in this stupid game, and he didn't even know why. Ethan could feel more tears coming along with his anger building up, but he took several deep breaths to regain control. There was no way he could help Maggie or anyone else by falling apart.

CHAPTER 12 - Seeker Secrets

"Over here," Drake called when Ethan and his friends walked into the Shadow Room. "And keep the lights off. No need to draw attention to ourselves."

Ethan squinted through the familiar dark room and scanned the computer tables. Everything was returned to the neat rows of tables and computers he remembered before their encounter with Gordy. After several minutes, Ethan's eyes adjusted to the darkness. Drake stood in front of one of the computers in the right-hand corner of the room along the same wall as the door. They walked hesitantly, half expecting Gordy to pop out of nowhere. The thought gave Ethan an eerie feeling as if they were being watched. He scanned the room for one of those security mirrors, but he didn't see any.

He scooted past his friends as an irresistible urge to shiver overtook him. *Yeah, this place is definitely giving me the creeps.* He kept moving, and when he finally made it across the room without incident, he breathed a sigh of relief.

When Ethan and his friends approached the computer, Drake had a list of files on the monitor. He turned the screen toward Ethan and the group and pointed to the long list of files. "These are the security files recorded from the mirrors. Those mirrors are what one would call a Smart

Mirror, meaning the mirror is not only a mirror and recording device, but an intelligent computer as well. The mirror works autonomously and in conjunction with these computers." Drake pointed around the room. "The artificial intelligence senses movements and voices, which triggers the monitoring feature of the mirrors. Then, they store them on these computers."

Ethan gasped. Mirrors that worked like computers? That was a first. "Are these files on every computer in here?" Ethan asked, glancing around the room.

Drake shook his head. "Just this one. And I can only access it and the files with my Guardian Key." He turned his attention back to the computer. "Show me the initial files."

The computer blinked to another screen that said: CONFIRM YOUR IDENTITY USING THE VERIFIER TO SWIPE YOUR KEY.

Drake removed the chain from his neck and flipped over the gold-lettered word "Guardian." He placed it on a nearby device that reminded Ethan of a scanner. The device lit up and took an image of the key.

"Thank you," a computerized female voice responded. "Please place your palm on the verifier." He placed it on the device, which emanated another white light. Ethan stared wide-eyed. He only read about devices like this in his favorite books. Once Drake obeyed the prompt, the screen blinked blue.

"Thank you," the voice said. "Access granted."

The monitor then switched to a screen with fewer files listed. He moved the computer mouse down the list until he came to a file labeled "Testing Seeker."

"Testing Seeker?" Brody asked. "What does that mean?"

Drake looked deep in thought for a minute, then turned to Brody. "Before the game went live, we had to test it."

"We?" Ethan asked. Did that mean Drake tested the game with Nith?

Drake nodded. "Let me show you." He double-clicked on the file, which opened a video. A boy about their age appeared on the video. He looked an awful lot like...

"Drake," Alyssa whispered. "You were there . . . but now here . . . what? How?" She stepped closer to the monitor.

Drake looked away again. "Yes. I was the first to test the game."

"Wait a second." Ethan held up a hand. "You're a game character, a part of the game. How can you test the game if you are part of it?"

"I wasn't always a part of the game. Just watch." He pointed to the video, which was already playing. Ethan and his friends exchanged looks, then turned their attention to the video.

Drake was at a level in the game Ethan didn't remember seeing yet. It looked like he failed to get a key. Shortly after, a figure appeared through purple swirling smoke. When the smoke cleared, the figure pointed his scepter at Drake's Transport, and then Drake disappeared. With that, the video went blank.

Ethan, Alyssa, Jason, and Brody stared in awe. It looked to Ethan like Drake was attacked by Nith. Worse, it looked like Drake was a player with a Transport at one time before being trapped. But why? "You—you're stuck in the game, too?" Ethan asked. "How did this happen?"

Drake stood and walked to the end of the table. He fidgeted with the edge of his shirt. "Like I said, I was the first to test the game. I disappeared there because I lost the level after making a deal with Nith. He had given me an extra life if I agreed that if I lost I would be bound to the game."

Alyssa lightly smacked Drake's arm. "Why would you do that? You're the one who tells us not to make deals."

He turned to her. "Yes, and this is why. When he said I'd be bound to the game, I thought what you and everyone else thinks: that this was just a game and so the threat wasn't real." He sighed. "But I was wrong. All of Nith's deals are traps. I trusted him. I never thought . . ." His voice trailed off. "When I lost that level after making the deal, I was not only trapped here, but Nith made me part of the game. He promised that if I was the guide, he'd free me after he traps enough people here."

"Woah." Ethan narrowed his eyes and closed in on Drake. "You traded other people's lives to save your own?"

Drake slapped his hands at his side and lifted his head to the ceiling. "It's not like I actually had a choice. Besides, I don't expect him to keep his word. You think he'll let me go with the popularity this game is getting?" He laughed darkly. "Yeah right. I'm as stuck as everyone else in here." He walked back to the computer and plopped in his seat.

"Well, we have no plans on Maggie staying stuck," Ethan said, "but I will free my sister from this monster."

"Yes, and I want to help you guys." Drake faced everyone and looked at each person in the room. "What Nith is doing is wrong. And the more power he gets, the worse he will be. I see that now."

"How is everyone getting stuck?" Brody asked. "Is it the same thing—by making deals?"

"Mostly," Drake said. "For some, though, they become addicted to the game. They play for longer and longer periods of time, and eventually they just never leave. The longer they stay, the more lost they are and the harder it is for them to stay away."

Ethan frowned. He could totally relate to that. It would have been so easy for it to happen to him. Then his thoughts turned to Maggie again. He couldn't think about her for long, though, because a loud bang echoed through the room, making him jump. "What was that?" He turned to see a chair had been knocked over. "Something's in here!"

Jason and Brody ran toward the sound at the other end of the room to investigate. Jason looked in the corners and Brody focused under the tables. Jason and Brody looked at each other.

Jason shook his head. "I don't see anything." As he finished speaking, a gust of air swooshed past him, causing his hair to move with the breeze. "Wow, but I felt that rush of air," Jason added. He held his arms close to himself and then smoothed his hair down.

"Gordy." Drake stood and glanced around the room. "I know it was him."

Alyssa nodded. "Who else can move that fast?"

"How much do you think he heard?" Ethan asked, eyeing the computer.

"Probably everything," Drake answered. "Gordy's hearing is as exceptional as his speed."

"Then we better jet," Brody said, making his way back to the front of the room.

As if on cue, the computer glitched and blinked until it finally went blank. Halfway across the room, a purple cloud of smoke sizzled in the air, twirling and swirling until it disappeared. Nith's beady black eyes stared at Ethan through the foggy room. He strode forward in slow steps, stopping in front of the group.

Nith pointed his scepter at Ethan. "So, we meet again." He

pulled his scepter back and admired the large purple orb. It looked much larger than the last time they encountered Nith. "It's pretty impressive, isn't it, how it grows." He held out the scepter. "Every time someone permanently joins our world, my power source grows. Which reminds me of the last time we met. What happened?" He twirled the staff in his hand. "Oh, that's right. You and 'Team Dynamite' were running for your lives." He pulled his gaze from his scepter and looked directly at Ethan.

Alyssa's face burned red. "We were *not* runni—"

Brody nudged her and shook his head.

"Yeah," Jason hissed. "Not the best time to pick a fight."

Ethan shook under Nith's unwavering stare, but he stood tall. He was not going to let Nith frighten him away again. Maggie was counting on him to get her out of here, and he had no intention of failing her.

"Oh, Jason, I think the fight is already picked." Ethan stepped forward without losing eye contact with Nith. "And we're not running this time."

Brody, Alyssa, and Jason joined Ethan, and the group stood tall together. After a long pause, Drake inched closer to the group and stood next to them. Relief and warmth flowed through Ethan. Up until then, he wasn't sure how much he could trust Drake. But now, with Drake standing by them, he had to know he was taking a stand—one which he might not survive.

With all of Team Dynamite with him—and now with a new team member—Ethan felt more confident. The group continued to hold Nith's stare, refusing to back down.

"Ohhhh. Isn't this sweet," Nith cooed. "Drake has become attached to this team." His eyes darkened and he aimed the scepter at Drake's chest. "I do not like traitors, no matter who they are."

CHAPTER 13 - The Prisoners

Drake backed up slowly. Nith followed. The orb on the scepter glowed purple, reflecting off of Drake's shirt.

Ethan's mind raced. *Quick . . . what should I do?* Nith's eyes narrowed, and Ethan realized that if he was going to help Drake, it had to be now. As Nith continued his advance, Ethan stuck his foot out, tripping Nith, then rushed over to Drake. Drake reached for the scepter but tripped, causing him to lose his chance of catching Nith off guard. The scepter fell to the floor and released a purple lightning bolt. Ethan and Drake darted out of the way, and Drake scurried behind one of the computers in the room. Alyssa, Brody, and Jason rushed to join Drake.

Drake stared at Nith with a knowing smile. "You don't want to hurt these bad boys, do you now?" Drake patted the computer in front of him.

Nith lowered his scepter.

"Oh, these must be important to you," Jason said with a grin. He headed over to another computer table.

Brody nodded in agreement and picked up a computer tower. He lifted it up to his chest and pretended to examine it. "I wonder what would happen . . ."

Ethan beamed. Of course. Even though the main computer had most of the files, the rest of them had to be important too. After all, they were hidden from the rest of the game. That gave him an idea. He ran to the end of the table and turned on one of the computers. If Nith wouldn't back off on his own, Ethan would have to encourage him.

He lifted the computer, holding it in front of him. The monitor remained on the table and displayed files listed as *Level 5 files.* He whistled to get Nith's attention. Nith spun around and gasped.

"Put that down," he roared.

Jason grinned and joined in. He picked up a computer labeled *Throne Room.* "Oh, should we choose this one?"

"You fools, these are not toys."

"Oh, man," Alyssa called from another corner of the room. "This is reallllly heavy." She held another computer and stumbled with an exaggerated buckling of the legs.

Ethan grinned and took a few steps closer to Nith. As he walked, the monitor, mouse, and keyboard trailed along the edge of the table.

"Stop!" Nith lowered his scepter.

Brody snuck behind Drake and walked along the shadows of the wall of the Shadow Room. *This is perfect,* Ethan thought to himself. *We've got Nith right where we want him.* "Drop the scepter."

Nith laughed a deep, evil laugh that echoed through the room. "Not a chance."

"Ohhhhh, I'm going to drop this computer aaannyyy second now," Alyssa called.

Ethan grinned. He loved her sassiness sometimes. "Drop it," he repeated to Nith.

Nith looked from Ethan to Jason—who was now balancing the computer with one hand high in the air—to Alyssa. Ethan gave Nith another pointed look.

"Okay," Nith roared and he threw the scepter to the ground.

Brody immediately emerged from the shadows and scooped up the scepter. Ethan nodded at Alyssa and Jason, who then set the computers down.

Jason circled the table. "I say we destroy these things anyway. Nith seems to need them for this game." He lifted his hand as if to swipe the table clean.

"Uh, I wouldn't do that," Drake called out with urgency in his voice. "You will trap us all and the people in the dungeon indefinitely."

Jason dropped his arms in defeat. "Too bad. I would have enjoyed destroying Nith's precious toys."

Ethan headed toward Nith and Brody. He wasn't sure what he was going to do with the scepter, but he would worry about that later. "You're going to free the people in the dungeon," Ethan commanded.

Nith shrugged his shoulders. "I'm sorry," he said, though Ethan could tell Nith was anything but sorry. "I need the scepter to do that." He blinked his eyes in a mockingly innocent way.

Ethan could feel his anger brewing again, but he took a deep breath. "Okay, then *we'll* do it." Even as the words left his mouth, he knew deep down it wasn't going to be that easy. When Nith laughed in response, it confirmed his fears.

Nith turned and clapped his hands twice. Instantly, Gordy appeared. He rushed at Brody and knocked him to the ground. Before Brody even hit the floor, Gordy had already pried Nith's scepter from Brody's hand and vanished. Though he did not appear to be in the room, Ethan had a feeling Gordy was still close by.

"Well, well, well, Ethan." Nith rubbed his hands together. "That was not a bad try from Team Dynamite."

Ethan glared in response.

"Perhaps we can be an even more powerful team. You're quite the leader, Ethan. People listen to you. You would be a very convincing apprentice of mine."

Now it was Ethan's turn to laugh, though he was definitely not amused.

"Now, don't be so quick to dismiss it." Nith stepped closer to Ethan. "There's great energy in you. You suppress it. Why?"

Ethan glared.

"Yes, yes." Nith smiled. "That's what I mean. We can be a great team. My power. Your emotional energy."

"Absolutely not." Ethan backed up several paces.

"Oh, I think your tune will change," Nith said and clapped his hands twice again. Gordy appeared, scepter still in his hands. Nith motioned for Gordy to approach him. Gordy obliged and bowed as his silvery long hair dangled before him. He reached out with the scepter and offered it to Nith. While still in the bow, Gordy turned his head slightly, just enough to catch Ethan's gaze. With a wink, he whispered, "The stick you find, do not leave behind." He then pulled out of the bow and stepped back. *What stick?* Ethan wondered. *What is he talking about?*

Before Ethan could utter a sound, Nith said, "Thank you, Gordy. You've been most helpful. For a change."

Ethan thought he saw Gordy respond with a scowl before he bowed and disappeared.

Nith turned to the group again. "Now, where were we?" He

tapped the side of his head as if he were solving the world's toughest puzzle. He snapped his fingers. "Oh, that's right. You all were about to join me in my quest."

Ethan pulled his friends behind him. Jason tried to get around him, but Ethan kept blocking him with his arms. He already had Max and Maggie trapped. He wasn't going to let Nith get his other friends too. Jason stood on his tiptoes and peered over Ethan's shoulders in response. Brody shook his head at Jason.

"No way," Ethan answered.

Nith moved closer to Ethan and circled the group while fingering the scepter. He eyed them up and down in eerie silence. "Such strong determination," he finally said. "We're a lot alike, you and I." He stopped circling them when he reached Ethan again.

"You know nothing about me."

"Oh no? I know you can't resist the pull of a good video game." Nith aimed his scepter at a computer which projected a video of Ethan in his living room playing Seeker while Maggie asked him to hang out with her. Ethan sucked in a breath as the image resurfaced the guilt he felt. Would it have been so hard for him to put the game down for a few hours?

Nith took a step closer to Ethan. Ethan's heart began to race.

"I know you adore her," Nith said, pointing to Maggie's image. He took another step closer.

Ethan tried to swallow the lump building up in his throat.

"And I know that your dad is not around. That's just another way we are alike." Nith let out another flash. An image appeared of the day Ethan's mom told him and Maggie that his dad had disappeared. Nith took another step closer. He now stood just inches away from Ethan.

Ethan's face burned with either irritation or sadness, he couldn't decide which. He always did his best to keep his deadbeat dad out of his thoughts, and he refused to think about it now.

Brody stepped in front of Ethan, forcing Nith to stumble back a few steps.

"How would you know about his dad?"

Ethan stood, unable to move. He didn't like thinking about his dad, knowing that he lived somewhere and still made no effort to see him or Maggie. The more his thoughts swirled in his head, the angrier he became. His dad was the last thing he wanted to think of. He snuck a peek behind him at Alyssa, who looked like she was going to cry.

"I told you before," Drake said, looking right at Brody. "He can hear you!"

Nith smiled his crooked smile. "You really should listen to Drake more." He pulled Drake from the group and dragged him next to himself. "He's been with me since the beginning."

"Yeah, so we heard," Jason piped up.

"None of this matters." Alyssa came out from behind Ethan. "We're not joining you."

Nith lifted his head so his purple hood just covered the tops of his eyes. "Suit yourself." He aimed his scepter toward the ceiling and shot a purple lightning bolt in the air. It hit the center of the ceiling and split into several smaller lightning bolts.

"Run," Ethan screamed, and he, Drake, Brody, Alyssa, and Jason scrambled away. The lightning bolts charged after them as if they had been programmed to hit each one of them. The lightning bolts caught up to them all at the same time and zapped at their Transports. Ethan's headset buzzed at the jolt.

Nith caught up with everyone as the glowing purple ball on his scepter seemed to grow by the minute.

"Uh, guys." Jason pointed to the orb. "Is that thing *growing*?"

Drake scowled. "Yes," he said through gritted teeth. "That means that while he was here with us, more and more people have been trapped in the dungeons." He stared directly at Nith. "His power grows and collects in that orb with each soul he traps." Drake pointed to the scepter.

"Yes," Nith's evil voice boomed. "They all think they can walk away from the game. Just one more play. One more life. One more minute. One more deal. All of it until their souls become mine."

Brody's face fell. Ethan was pretty sure he knew what Brody was thinking. Maggie was part of the purple energy now. "It's okay," he mouthed. He couldn't think about that now. He had seen her. Maggie was just sleeping.

"My lightning bolts, powered by the collection of souls, are very powerful . . . and they follow my every command. They went straight for your headsets, did they not?" Nith tilted his head in a questioning stance. "And now your headsets will no longer transport you anywhere outside of this game. Instead"—he aimed at their headsets again—"Gordy planned a little fun for you. Let's see if it changes your minds."

Nith released the lightning bolts, and they zapped at their heads. A bright light flashed, and when it faded, Ethan was no longer in the Shadow Room.

Instead, walls of towering hedges surrounded him. Just a few feet in front of him stood a tall leafy archway that stretched above the hedges. A narrow path waited ahead. Ethan's mouth went dry.

He swallowed hard. A large sign floated above the arch with

the message, “Welcome to The Snare. A truly *captivating* maze.”

CHAPTER 14 - The Snare

Ethan stepped forward with hesitation. *Where is everyone?* There was no sign of Brody, Alyssa, Jason, or Drake. That couldn't be good news.

He eyed the narrow pathway, trying to decide if he should wait for his friends. After several minutes of not hearing from anyone, he decided to go looking for them. He remembered reading about people getting stuck in mazes. He'd have to find a way to ensure he wasn't running in circles. He walked to the end of the pathway and turned right. As soon as he did, he tore off a branch from the hedges, causing an indentation in the leafy wall. He continued to do that with each turn he made, hoping it was enough to stop him from going down the same pathways.

He moved quicker as he fell into a routine of making turns and tearing branches. He continued along until he tripped over a thick tree root emerging from the ground. He reached out to catch his fall just before his face would have smashed into the dirt. He stood and dusted himself off.

He took a few steps forward but froze when something zipped by him. Then, just as quickly, Gordy appeared in front of him. Ethan groaned. "Oh, not you again!"

"Oh, come on," Gordy taunted as he lifted himself in the air.

"Aren't you up for a little fun?" Gordy smiled. With a snap of his fingers, and a wink for good measure, the bushes on both sides of Ethan grew taller and taller. As they moved up, they moved toward each other until they intertwined. The two bushes twisted tighter to form the shape of a very tall monster. Shock raged through Ethan as the tree monster stretched out an arm, made a fist, then plummeted it down to the ground. The bushes rustled loudly, and the force of the blow shook the ground as Monster Bush made an impact and blocked Ethan's path.

Roots from the same bushes grew wider and thicker until they resembled the trunk of a large old oak tree. The growing stopped and Ethan breathed a sigh of relief—until the roots pulled from the ground. With one giant tug, the roots tore out of the earth. They twisted and stretched until they formed two wooden feet.

Ethan gulped. This Monster Bush now had feet. Feet that could make it move. *Great.* That was just what Ethan needed: a moving, thinking, fighting beast. It turned toward him and cleared the path between them. Ethan ran forward, taking his chance. He advanced several feet before—*bang*! Leafy branches from the bush, which now looked like large fists, punched the ground and cut him off.

How am I going to get past that thing? If only I had something to fight it off with. He scurried behind Monster Bush, looking for anything he could find. Monster Bush twisted to follow Ethan. One of the thinner roots at the bush's feet snapped in half. Ethan grabbed one end and pulled. It didn't budge. He stood in front of the root and pulled again with all his might, trying to snap it off. Monster Bush bent down with its leafy fist and flicked the root.

Crrraaack! The root snapped with Ethan still holding on. He and the root flew backwards. He flipped through the air at least seven times before he landed on his elbows. He scrambled back to his feet, a little off-balance, with the stick in hand. His stinging elbow throbbed, but he ignored it. Monster Bush was charging his way. Ethan squinted to gain a better focus of the scene spinning in front of him.

A large figure—Monster Bush—came into clearer focus as it advanced on Ethan, whose pulse raced as panic set in. Ethan looked at the stick in his hand. It would be a miracle if it helped him in any way. But then he remembered Gordy's words from the Shadow Room: "The stick you find, do not leave behind." Still unsure of what Gordy meant, he figured it couldn't hurt to keep the stick, especially considering the massive figure was now in front of him. Monster Bush swiped at Ethan. He ducked, crouching to the ground, but still caught a few branches against his cheek. He felt the warm trickle of blood and wiped it away with the back of his hand.

He looked to the left of him. Large boulders surfaced through the dirt where the bush was once planted. Maybe he could use those to disable the bush. He ran over to them and set down his stick. He pulled with all his strength and rolled the large boulder forward. When it moved, it exposed several smaller rocks hidden under the big rock.

Monster Bush came back at Ethan, ready for another swipe. Ethan reached for one of the smaller rocks and threw it. That wasn't effective as the branches absorbed the rock. He threw more and more, but it didn't faze Monster Bush. Instead, it further angered him. Monster Bush charged forward, coming within inches of Ethan. Ethan dropped the stones and picked up his stick again. He swung at Monster Bush. The beast jumped back enough for Ethan to get past him and run to the end of the passageway. He turned around in time to see Monster Bush still on his trail. He held the stick defensively in front of himself like a sword. Toward the bottom of the stick, Ethan noticed something etched into the wood. He peered closer and saw the shape of a horse—no, it had wings. It wasn't a horse. It was a dragon. "Flutter," Ethan said, his voice just above a whisper. He ran his fingers over the carving. Maybe this was more than just a stick. "Okay. Let's see what this thing can do," he said.

Ethan didn't know if the stick actually heard him or not, but it grew warm in his hands. He glanced at the dragon etching, which glowed white. The rest of the stick became warmer and warmer until it glowed bright yellow. Beams of golden light emerged from every angle of the stick.

Ethan was so shocked that he came close to dropping the stick. Monster Bush must have been surprised as well, for it stopped in its tracks. The stick continued to glow yellow, but the yellow glow merged with the white glow. As the lights touched, the stick twisted and morphed. The top of it stretched into a wide and pointy edge. The bottom of the stick had loose bark that braided itself around the edges, forming a sturdy wooden handle. Right at the base of the sword sat a more defined carving of the dragon. What he held in his hand was no longer a stick. It was a sturdy sword.

"Woah," he whispered. He didn't know how it happened, but he now had a fighting chance. Monster Bush recovered from the shock as well and was now back to rushing at Ethan. As soon as it got close enough to him, Ethan swung his sword. He wasn't prepared for how heavy it would feel when he swung, and it showed. Instead of a crisp, even swing, the sword wobbled in his hands. He juggled with it, and when Monster Bush took a swing at him, he clumsily blocked the branches with his sword. He swung again. This time, he had a much more controlled swing. The sword cut through the arm-shaped branches and they dropped to the ground.

Monster Bush retreated briefly, but missing arm or not, the bush was not stopping. It charged again at Ethan. It swung its only remaining arm, striking Ethan's shoulder. Ethan flew sideways and landed on his side. In his fall, he lost the sword. Monster Bush noticed too and they both dived for it. Monster Bush was faster and swiped the sword.

Ethan raced back to the other end of the passage where the boulders sat. He picked up several of the surrounding rocks and fired them at Monster Bush one after the other. Whiz! Whiz! Whiz! Monster Bush easily absorbed the rocks within its leaves and responded with a guttural roar. Ethan grabbed more rocks. Two of them were swallowed up by Monster Bush. It was no use. Monster Bush kept absorbing them. The beast strutted toward Ethan. Closer and closer it got until Ethan had no other options left. He took a chance and hurled his last rock at the sword.

Thunk.

The rock hit the sword and flung it out of Monster Bush's hand. The sword landed to the left. Ethan lunged for his sword. His fingers curled around the braided handle, and he picked it up with trembling hands.

Monster Bush charged at Ethan. It swung at Ethan's shoulder once more. This time Ethan was ready. He side-stepped backwards and turned his body away from Monster Bush. Then he spun in a circle and slashed at Monster Bush's other arm. Swoosh.

Monster Bush's arm broke free and fell to the ground.

Monster Bush fell backwards, exposing its roots. Ethan quickly rushed after it. As Monster Bush struggled, armless, to get up, Ethan hoped he could stop the battle before any more damage would occur.

"C'mon, Monster Bush," he called. "We don't have to fight. Just stop." But Monster Bush would have none of that. It tore off a branch and swung at Ethan's leg. The rough stick made contact, cutting him deep. Then, Monster Bush lifted its root-leg at Ethan, ready to swing again. Ethan blocked the blow with his sword just as contact was made.

Monster Bush rolled over, still thrashing and kicking. Ethan stepped on a root to keep it still, but Monster Bush was able to kick him away. The beast inched toward Ethan and hunched over him. Ethan swung and swung at the roots. "C'mon, I know we can do it," he whispered to his sword. He brushed his fingers against the dragon etching.

The sword grew warm and glowed yellow once again. Monster Bush squinted at the light. Ethan took his chance! He jumped to his feet and swung at Monster Bush. His glowing sword made contact and sliced through the thickest root. Monster Bush roared as it crashed to the ground one final time. It fell silent and motionless.

Ethan sat back, trembling and not believing that he survived. He took several deep breaths to regulate his breathing. His thoughts, no longer racing a mile a minute, slowed to normal. Now that he was calm, he set out to find his friends. However, the thought of them worried him. If he had that encounter with the Monster Bush, the others were probably dealing with something just as deadly. He had to find them—and fast.

CHAPTER 15 - Dynamite Reunited

Ethan opened his inventory and placed the sword inside one of the blank spaces. Next, he hopped over the scattered leaves and branches and set out to find his friends. He ventured farther into the maze, continuing through the bushes until he came to a fork in the path. Unsure of which way his friends could be, he cupped his hands around his mouth and called, "Brody. Alyssa. Jason. Drake. Anyone there?" No response. He turned left and ran faster. The path stretched endlessly. He ran and ran, calling out his friends' names every few steps. Still, there was no sign of them.

He continued to run, bringing on an achy sensation in his legs. As he continued, the feeling turned to a burning sensation. He stopped to catch his breath, bending over slightly and resting his hands on his thighs. He rubbed them gently until the burning subsided. He looked ahead. Another turn sat ready at the end of the pathway. He straightened and then raced toward it. As he ran, he didn't see a pile of branches that sat to the side. His foot collided with it and he tumbled to the ground, scraping his elbows.

"Ouch." This maze was really beating him up.

"Ethan?"

Ethan straightened. Was that Brody? "Brody? Over here."

The boys kept calling to each other until Brody finally rounded the corner at the end of the pathway. Ethan raced the rest of the way to meet him.

"You're alone too?" Ethan asked as nobody else followed Brody around the corner.

Brody nodded. "It looks like we were all separated."

"Okay, let's keep looking."

They turned the corner where Brody came from and continued forward, calling out to their friends. After some time of searching, Ethan heard a yell to the left. Ethan and Brody turned down the passage, where a thin stream of smoke hung in the sky. They rushed forward until they found Jason against a bushy wall halfway down the passage. He had scratches on his arm while the wall sat singed and smoking.

Ethan and Brody exchanged worried looks. "Jason!" Brody called as they rushed toward him.

Jason waved his hand. "Sweet! I was hoping I wasn't the only one lost in here."

"Do we even want to know what happened here?" Ethan asked, surveying the damage. As he looked closer, there were several singed bushes around the area. One burnt bush had a perfect outline the size and shape of a gnome, right down to his pointy hat.

Jason grinned. "Pffft. Nothing I can't handle. That gnomey was no match for this homey!" He pointed to his chest, then flexed his biceps for emphasis.

Ethan groaned.

Brody shook his head and grinned. "That was an excruciating sentence to hear."

Jason rubbed Brody's brown hair. "Aww, don't be jealous."

A loud shriek stopped everyone in their tracks.

"That sounds like Alyssa," Ethan said and ran toward the scream. He motioned for everyone to follow as he raced to the end of the passageway.

As Ethan reached the end, Alyssa's voice grew louder. "Oh, no you don't. You will not get my ring!"

Ethan froze. "It sounds like they're after her ring again. C'mon, she might be in trouble."

Wrestling and scuffling sounds filled the air from the other side of the hedges. A loud "Woooaaaaaahhhhhh" rang out followed by a swoosh from the bushes.

Ethan, Jason, and Brody turned the corner, which led them into a large, open, square area.

"This must be the center of the maze," Brody said.

To the left hung a gnome, stuck face-first into the bushy wall with his tiny wiggling butt sticking out. At first, Ethan thought it was Gordy, but this one's hair didn't have as much silver in it as Gordy's. He stopped wiggling after a few minutes and his little feet dangled helplessly behind him in defeat.

Jason walked up to it grinning. "Aww. Look. He's stuck." He lifted the gnome's foot and let go. It bounced off the hedge. Lots of loud muffled words emerged from the direction of the bush.

Ethan looked over to see Alyssa standing proud with her hands on her hips and Drake right next to her. "I warned him not to mess with me and my grandma's ring."

"Dude, it was hilarious," Drake said. He motioned his hands in all directions with mock punches and kicks for effect. "First she did this. Then this. And pow." He pointed back where the gnome was still stuck.

Ethan pulled the gnome out of the bush. Maybe it could answer some questions for him. But as soon as he did, it vanished. Ethan shrugged. "Looks like he had enough humiliation for one day."

"And what happened to you guys?" Alyssa asked.

Ethan pulled out his wooden sword and filled Alyssa in on his battle with Monster Bush and Jason's encounter with his gnome.

Alyssa whistled. "We really are Team Dynamite!"

Drake nodded and looked serious. "I had a feeling about this group, which is why I opened up more with you guys." He ran his fingers through his hair and sighed. "Speaking of which, we should be very close to the exit of the maze, but I know our battles are not finished. When Nith destroyed your Transports, he wanted to ensure that you would never escape the game."

Brody stepped forward. "So how do we escape then? Keep going room to room?"

"And don't forget about Maggie and Max," Ethan said.

Drake nodded. "We keep going. There are several more levels ahead of us, and the only way to leave this game now is to confront Nith . . . and win. But he won't make it easy. Like I said before, you changed the game when you got Nith's attention. And with him, anything can happen." He sighed. "No matter who you are to him."

Ethan's heart sank. He only wanted to find Maggie and Max and get home. He was starting to wish he never got the Transport or downloaded Seeker. Maybe if he hadn't played so much or ignored Maggie, she wouldn't be in this situation—trapped in a virtual nightmare—which was all the more reason he had to get her out of there.

"Let's get going, then," Ethan said. He moved to the middle of the square. In each of the four walls bordering the square, there was an arch-shaped opening that led to more passageways.

"Which exit do we take?" Brody asked, taking a moment to eye each arch. "I know it's not the way Ethan, Jason, and I came." He pointed behind them.

"And it's not that way," Alyssa said, pointing directly across from the opening Brody and Ethan had come through. "That's where I came through."

"And I came from there." Drake pointed to the right.

"Okay, so that leaves the left," Brody said.

"And everyone is sure there wasn't an exit behind them?" Ethan looked at all his friends.

Jason nodded. "Yeah, at least I am. One minute there was that blinding light that Nith was so kind to expose us to." He rolled his eyes. "The next, I'm plopped in a far corner of the maze. No turning back—the only way I could go was forward."

Everyone nodded in agreement. "Okay," Ethan said, "it looks like we go left, then."

The group made their way out of the square to the left. Alyssa and Ethan led in the front followed by Brody, Jason, and Drake. Ethan tried not to think about how Maggie was doing so he could concentrate on getting to her as fast as possible, but it was hard to do. *I shouldn't have ignored her. Then she wouldn't be stuck in this mess.*

Alyssa reached for Ethan's hand. "She's going to be okay."

Ethan watched the ground as they kept walking. "I hope so. I'll never forgive myself if—"

Alyssa squeezed his hand. "Stop. Be strong for her. If we stay stuck in the past, succeeding in the future will be impossible." She looked down. "That's something my grandmother used to always say." She took a deep breath. "Anyway, if we focus on helping Maggie, I'm sure we'll get there."

They walked a short distance further and came to another

fork in the path.

"Right or left?" Alyssa asked.

Ethan thought for a minute, remembering that Alyssa had come from the part of the maze that was to their right.

"What do you think?" he asked. "Left again?"

"I say right," Brody said.

At once several arguments erupted. Half of the group thought they should go with what had been successful thus far, and the other half, including Drake, was convinced the group should try right.

Eventually, they all settled on turning right. Ethan sighed. If Drake was convinced . . . however, he couldn't shake the nagging feeling that they were heading toward disaster.

"For the record," Ethan said, "I have a bad feeling about this."

He took a deep breath as he and Alyssa led the group to the right.

CHAPTER 16 - The Key

They followed the path to the end and rounded the corner. The trail ahead stretched on and they turned to the left. Then it went straight again. Alyssa slowed her pace and chewed her fingernail. "This is looking familiar to me."

They continued on until the path veered to the right. Ethan's mind wandered as they walked. He thought of Maggie sleeping in that dungeon. If only he had kept his promise, maybe she wouldn't be there. He let out a sigh and kicked a pebble.

Alyssa's voice echoed in his head. "Focus on the future." He was trying—really, he was—but guilt was a monster of its own, one that seemed much bigger than Monster Bush.

Brody gently tapped Ethan on the arm with the back of his hand. "You okay?"

Ethan looked at the ground. "Yeah. I just wish Maggie—"

Alyssa stopped and faced Ethan. "Hey. We'll get her out of here. Focus on that." She gave him a pointed look.

Ethan wasn't convinced, but he nodded.

The group moved forward and the path twisted and turned, turning right, then left, then right again. By this time, Ethan lost track of where they were. He stopped and turned to the group. "Maybe we should head back and go the other way.

I feel like we're running in circles."

Alyssa stomped her foot. "I knew this looked familiar." She pointed straight ahead. "Isn't that the center of the maze where we were before?" Sure enough, in the far distance at the end of the passage was an arch that led to the opening of the grassy square.

The group rushed over. Yep. It was definitely the same spot because the gnome-shaped hole in the bush across the square sat exactly as they had left it several minutes earlier.

As they entered the square, a flash of light appeared with the gnome Ethan freed earlier, and he looked a whole lot less humiliated. He hung in the air, levitating with an evil grin and revenge in his eyes.

Alyssa rolled up her sleeves. "Back for more, I see?"

"Ohhh, burn," Jason said and doubled over for effect.

"I'd be de-*light*-ed," the gnome answered and snapped his fingers. A purple beam of light appeared in the air. It split into four smaller ones and landed at each arch in the square, blocking all the exits to the rest of the maze. When Ethan tried to touch the purple wall of light, it threw him backward with such force he hit the ground, landing on his back. The light remained stationary, like a force-field, under each arch, trapping everyone inside.

"Great, thanks, Alyssa," Brody said and rolled his eyes.

"How are we going to get out of here?" Ethan said, eyeing every inch he could of the closest arch. "How do you dismantle light?"

"The gnome is the source of the light," Drake said. "It's his power keeping it there."

"So, we need to take down the gnome," Brody said and eyed the creature.

Ethan scanned the bushes and the ground for rocks, sticks—anything he could use to disable the gnome. He thought about using the sword, but he wanted something to knock the gnome out of the air first. Brody was already over by one of the walls rummaging through the bush. He turned and tossed Ethan a rock, then Alyssa, Jason, and Drake.

Ethan held out his rock and lined it up with the gnome. He wound his arm back and hurled the rock forward through the air with all his strength. The rock hit the gnome's arm but he remained unscathed in the air. "Ooh." He rubbed his hands together. "Dodgeball. I'm pretty good at that." To illustrate his point, he weaved through the air, quickly changing directions. He jumped to the left, then the right, and finished with a backflip before floating back in place.

Alyssa, Jason, and Drake peppered the gnome with rocks anyway, despite the gnome's quick maneuvers. It dodged Each and every one! Alyssa threw her arms in the air in frustration. "It's no use."

When she did, light from one of the archways reflected off of her ring. Ethan thought the light blinded the gnome for a second as it shielded its eyes. However, the light never reached the gnome's eyes. Instead, it caught his exposed pinky finger, which instantly changed to . . .

"Stone?" Jason asked. "Cool!"

The gnome howled in anger.

"Wait." Ethan rushed to Alyssa's side. "Do that again."

"Do what? Throw my hands in the air?" She repeated the gesture.

Again, the purple light hit her ring in a perfect spot, which reflected onto the gnome's whole hand. This time, his entire hand turned to stone, and the gnome scowled. He zipped in the air to the other side of the square, though he was much slower with the weight of his hardened hand.

A look of realization hit Alyssa. "Quick." She pointed to everyone. "If you have anything reflective on you at all—belt, chain, mirror—"

"Mirror?" everyone cried in unison. Whatever made Alyssa think three boys would carry a mirror was beyond them.

She threw her head back dramatically. "Whatever! Find something and get ready."

Ethan ripped off the zipper from one of his boots. Jason tore the metal buckle off his belt. Drake ripped off his chain with the tag that read "Guardian of Bailiwick." Brody had nothing.

"Wait," Alyssa said. "I probably do actually have a mirror on me." She reached in her pocket and pulled out a compact mirror. She grinned and tossed it to Brody.

Ethan smiled at her. "Well, I gotta hand it to you. You're always prepared."

She blushed and then said with a slight nod, "You know it."

Now that everyone had something reflective, Ethan and Alyssa directed everyone to stand in a semicircle facing one of the walls of light. Alyssa held her ring out first, which reflected a beam. The gnome moved to dodge it and laughed.

"We need everyone to do this at once," Ethan said. This time everyone held out their reflectors. The purple light bounced off of each reflector, splitting the light beam into several fragments. The fragments bounced off each other and shot around the square. Several beams hit the gnome one after another.

"Keep going," Brody called out.

More light reflected and split, showering the gnome with endless light beams. As they did, more and more of the gnome turned to stone. One final light beam bounced off of the mirror Brody held and zapped the gnome in the heart. The remainder of the gnome slowly turned to stone.

Everyone lowered their reflectors and the light beams stopped shooting. When the last bit of the gnome turned to stone, the purple walls of light vanished.

"Huh." Jason slapped a hand on Ethan's back. "Taking out the gnome with his own magic. Sweet!"

"Very resourceful," Drake agreed as he reattached his chain.

Several minutes later, the group left the center of the maze. This time when they reached the fork in the passageway, they turned left. Ethan pulled his wooden sword out from his boot.

Jason gave him a puzzled look.

"What?" Ethan asked. "Based on our experiences in this maze, I'm going to be ready for whatever surprises come our way."

But the group didn't run into any more surprises. When they turned to the left, they only had a short way to go. They followed a few twists and turns before turning down a long pathway. The path stretched on a good way down, but at the end, there was a rectangular doorway instead of all the arched doorways in the rest of the maze. When they reached the doorway, an illuminated message hung in the air that read, "Congratulations on escaping the maze." The group moved past the sign and through the doorway.

As soon as they did, Ethan's wooden sword grew warm again. He rested it in the middle of both hands and held it in front of him.

"What in the—" Jason started. He and the rest of Team Dynamite stared in awe.

The sword grew warmer and warmer in Ethan's hands,

glowing with a yellow halo. He could almost feel the power radiating off of it. The sword lifted off his hands, glowing even further. It twisted, pulled, and changed shape. It grew smaller and smaller until it was only a few inches long. It continued to morph its shape until it resembled a golden key. Then it gently landed back in Ethan's hands.

CHAPTER 17 - Distraction

"Woah." Jason picked up the key and held it in front of him. He turned it in his hand a few times, examining each side. The group approached the metal door separating the maze from the castle entrance. The key glowed and Ethan held it up to the door. The door beeped and slid open. Then, just as quickly, the key turned back into the sword. Ethan waved his hand and the inventory box appeared. The sword floated to its box before the inventory vanished.

Ethan was the first to walk past the door and into the new area. It was a large, open dining room. A mahogany dining table extended more than half the length of the room. Ethan guessed it could easily fit thirty people. The edges of the table were outlined in gold and the tabletop reflected the light from the three-tiered crystal chandeliers above it. Three pedestal bases supported the table off of the glistening white floor. Five simple wall lights hung on the wall across the table, spaced evenly apart. A wide-open rectangular doorway rested in the lower right-hand corner of the wall. Ethan craned his neck to see behind the doorway, which looked like a corridor to the kitchen. Against the opposite wall was a mahogany hutch that matched the table. On one side were several water jugs.

On the other side, glistening silver utensils rested in a wooden box lined with a red velvety interior. Next to it rested a closed smaller rectangular box that Ethan assumed was another fancy accessory for the table.

"Before we go any further," Brody said as he ran his fingers along the smooth tabletop, "we need to figure out where to go from here." He looked around the room. "There has to be several rooms in this place."

Drake nodded. "Countless."

Ethan stomped a foot. "Maggie could be anywhere. We don't have time for that."

Alyssa walked over to him and laid her hand on his arm. "We'll figure it out."

His heart swelled in response to her touch, and warmth filled his body. He smiled, and for the first time, he felt more in control of his frustrations. "Thank you," he whispered.

Drake coughed. "Well, it's good you have someone with you who's been part of the game from the beginning."

Jason tilted his head to one side. "Have you been holding out on us again?"

"Absolutely not." Drake grinned. "But I've been around long enough to observe the layout of the fortress and how the game was designed to work. I created a map a while ago." He signaled his inventory and swiped several times to the left. In the top corner was a parchment paper icon labeled *Bailiwick Map*. "Not much was going on here when I first got stuck, so I would draw. At first, it was random things, but as I made my way around, I took note of where all the rooms were so I could get where I needed to be quickly."

Ethan recalled all of the times Drake showed up out of the blue, usually scaring the life out of them.

"Wait," Brody said. "Didn't you have a map of the maze too?"

Drake shook his head. "I only have a map of the rooms in the castle and the path to The Keep. In fact, I don't recall much about a maze at all. It's almost as if it's . . . new."

Ethan crinkled his eyebrows. *Why would the maze just appear out of nowhere?* Again, Gordy's words echoed in his head. "The stick you find, do not leave behind." *If the maze just appeared, how would Gordy even know about the stick?*

Brody interrupted Ethan's train of thought and nodded in Drake's direction. "So that map should show us the way to the holding cell where Max and Maggie are."

Drake nodded.

Ethan frowned. The thought of Maggie as a prisoner made him shudder. *Though, knowing Maggie, she won't make this easy for Nith if she can help it. That is, if she is even awake.*

"Does every room have a key?" Alyssa asked Drake.

He flipped his head back, and his long bangs swished to the side. "No. Only the rooms that would have led you to the next level. I imagine that even though the game changed, Nith probably kept those doors in as security."

He walked to the far end of the dining room and examined the doorway. It looked like an ordinary door until Drake reached out to push it. The disguise lifted and revealed the metal door.

"Yep," Drake called as he made his way back to the group. "Just as I thought. Nith isn't going to make things easy for us to get around. Besides, I assume he needs a lot to stay in place so he can continue to trap more gamers."

A loud crash interrupted their conversation followed by Gordy's high-pitched voice. Ethan arched his eyebrows and turned toward the sound. Gordy was balancing three large plates in the palm of one hand. A fourth plate sat shattered on the dining room table. "I thought that might get your attention," he chortled. The plates had purple and yellow wavy lines circling the edge. A purple and white marbled circle sat in every dip of the wavy lines. *Nith sure has a lot of purple things,* Ethan thought.

"What do you want?" Brody said through gritted teeth. "Haven't you and your gnome friends had enough?"

Gordy waved a hand at Brody. "Oh, the fun's just beginning. Here. Catch!" Gordy tossed the plate like a frisbee toward Brody's head. Jason must have sensed that Gordy was about to throw something because just as the plate left Gordy's hand, Jason lunged for Brody and tackled him to the ground. Both boys immediately scrambled back to their feet.

More plates whizzed by, aimed at Drake, Brody, Ethan, Alyssa, and Jason. Ethan raced to the table to grab Gordy's foot, but Gordy levitated in the air and dangled out of his reach. Ethan jumped and jumped, swiping the air with each leap, but he missed Gordy every time. He paused, leaning on the table to catch his breath, and looked to the left. Something shiny was on the corner of the table. He rushed over and picked up what he could now see was a silver tray. On the tray were five rings, much like the laser rings from the library level. He quickly tossed everyone a ring. They placed the ring on their fingers. Alyssa was careful to use the hand her grandmother's ring wasn't on. The friends stood in a line and aimed the laser ring at Gordy. The six separate lasers merged into one as they reached Gordy.

Ethan expected the laser to send Gordy hurling across the room and hopefully far away, but when the laser hit him, it went right through him as if he were a ghost.

The laser then struck the wall, leaving a singed hole.

Gordy did a backflip in the air and laughed. "That was a cute try," he taunted. He snapped his fingers and more plates appeared. *Hundreds* of plates appeared.

One by one they rose in the air. There were so many floating, Ethan could barely see Gordy on the other side. Once they reached above Gordy's head, they began pummeling toward Ethan and the rest of his friends.

Soon they were dodging left. Then right. Then up. Then down.

"Split up," Ethan yelled, and everyone scattered behind different parts of the table. It wasn't an ideal choice, but it was the best they had considering the room they were in.

Using a chair for cover, Ethan peered out and aimed his laser ring at the plates charging in his direction. He hit the plates one after the other, shattering them before they could slam into him.

The battle raged on as Ethan and his friends took on an endless stream of murderous plates. One plate headed straight for Alyssa's head and Ethan thought Alyssa saw it too late to duck or dodge it. He was about to shoot it away from her when one headed right for him. As he fought off another shower of attacks, he expected to hear Alyssa cry out, but she never did. He peeked over and saw her just standing there, not moving as more plates scattered around her.

"Stop." Alyssa cupped her hands to her mouth. "Stop shooting, guys."

There was no way Ethan was going to stop. He was sure they were getting to the end of plates. They had to be. They'd been fighting forever.

"Ohhh," Drake said, dropping his ring and joining Alyssa.

"I should have known."

Brody and Jason soon joined them.

"What the heck, guys?" Were they seriously leaving all the fighting to him? He could feel his frustration surfacing, but he pushed it deep down. He didn't have time to worry about that now as all the plates were focused on him. There should have been much less than what was coming at him, and it was getting hard to fight them all off.

Alyssa, Brody, Jason, and Drake rushed over to the dining room hutch. Ethan couldn't imagine why . . . he was still fighting for his life. His frustration returned and his heart raced. "*Come on*. I need some help here."

Finally, the flow of plates slowed and Ethan could see Gordy lounging on the table. He continued shooting at the plates. He was sure after he destroyed the last few he'd be finished. Only a little left.

A light touch pulled him out of his trance. "Ethan," Alyssa said. "Stop."

"What do you mean? We're almost through this." He ducked to dodge another plate. "Well. *I'm* almost through this." *Seriously why is nobody helping me?*

"Did ya notice you're the only one with plates hurling your way?" Alyssa tilted her head and raised her eyebrows.

What is she talking about? He shook his head as another plate headed his way. Zap. It split into pieces.

"Ethan. It's a distraction. We've been shooting *forever*. Watch." She jumped in front of him as plates raced toward them.

Ethan lunged for her and tossed her aside. "Are you insane?" Then he turned and focused back on the challenge at hand. Alyssa sighed, turned to Brody, and said, "I give up. You try."

Still, Ethan couldn't pull his gaze away from the scene in front of him.

"Yo, man," Brody called. "You have to stop. Just. Stop."

"But they're almost gone." Ethan's hands shook as more plates suddenly joined the attack. "Uuuugh."

Brody laid a hand on Ethan's shoulder. "We don't have to fight the plates. I'm telling you."

Ethan jerked his shoulder away, never taking his eyes off the plates. "Yes, we do. A little more and then I think we're good."

"Want me to tackle him and grab the ring?" Jason asked. He assumed a position you'd see a football player take.

Brody sighed. "I didn't want to do this, but I think it's the only way to get you to snap out of it." He took a deep breath. "Remember why we're here."

Ethan slowed his firing at the plates but still fended them off.

Brody took another step toward him. "Alyssa's right. This is a distraction. We need to get to Max." He paused. "And Maggie."

Ethan's heart felt like it stopped. Maggie. But he was doing this for Maggie.

Alyssa jumped in front of him again, this time holding something in her hands. "We have the key. We can move on."

Ethan completely stopped his firing. As he did, the remaining plates zoomed toward him. When they were supposed to slam into him, they went right through him and vanished.

His mouth dropped open and he looked at where Gordy was still lounging on the table. Gordy stood, waved, and then disappeared.

"It was an illusion," Drake said, moving to a spot next to Alyssa.

Ethan trembled. "How–how long have we–I been doing this?" He looked at each of his friends. They all exchanged uncomfortable looks, and Ethan decided that was all the information he needed.

"Are we done wasting time now?" Jason asked. He smirked, but his eyes were serious.

Alyssa grabbed Ethan's arm. "C'mon. Let's go."

"Wait." Jason ran to the hutch and grabbed the jugs of water and stashed them in his inventory. "Okay. We're good now."

Alyssa and Ethan walked ahead of the rest of the group toward the metal door at the far end of the dining room. "Thank you for listening," Alyssa whispered. She turned to him. "I know it was hard for you to walk away from that challenge with the plates. That challenge had a strong hold on you."

Ethan stared at his feet. "I couldn't stop. It felt like I would have had those plates taken care of. But right when I thought I was done, more and more appeared."

Alyssa tucked one of her long brown curly locks behind her ear. "I thought so too . . . until one of the plates went right through me. Then, I knew. The plates were designed to keep us focused on them and distracted from our real purpose."

Drake caught up with them. "Yeah, when I realized what was going on, I checked the hutch. And sure enough, the key was in that small rectangular box."

Ethan's heart sank. They had the key the *whole* time. They could have been so much further along in the quest had he not been playing with flying plates.

"Don't worry." Alyssa started walking again. "You pulled out of it. You came through. Now . . . we move on."

Ethan nodded, but he was deeply disturbed. He let the game consume him so much that it could have cost him his sister . . . and even all of their lives.

He drew a deep breath. *No more,* he promised himself. *No. More. Distractions.*

CHAPTER 18 - The Mirror

"Great, more mirrors," Jason said as they entered another long hallway. They had just swiped their key at the steel door, and Ethan had expected another large room. Apparently, Jason had too. Instead, a vast hallway greeted them. Black and grey tiled floors sat in a checkered pattern as far as Ethan could see. Security mirrors were lined evenly along the walls.

Ethan and his friends walked and walked, but the hallway seemed to go on forever. Silence followed them down the hall. The only noise heard were the clicks and shuffles of their footsteps.

"This isn't right." Ethan stopped and examined one of the mirrors. His finger traced the rippled silver frame.

Alyssa flipped her brown curls behind her shoulder. "You're right. It's never this quiet here."

"Or this easy." Jason pointed his finger to nobody in particular.

Ethan turned to Drake. "Do you think this passageway is a trick?"

Drake crinkled his nose. "I don't think so. I mean, all the other keys led to the next level of the game."

Ethan shrugged. That was true. And with each room they

went through, they were that much closer to getting Maggie back. His heart sank. He wondered what she was doing. *Is she still unconscious? Is she hurt?*

He walked over to one of the security mirrors. He tapped the glass, and his reflection faded away, leaving only clear ripples. "Show me Maggie."

Nothing happened.

Ethan gathered all the power he could behind his voice and tried again. "Show me Maggie."

Drake walked over, shaking his head. "It's a *security* mirror, Ethan. Only Nith and I can access them."

"Wait." Brody held up his hand. "How do you still have access? I mean, I'm pretty sure Nith revoked that access once he tossed us all in the maze."

Drake grinned and held up his Guardian of Bailiwick chain. "I'm sure he did, but I've been working a long time to get out of here. Long before you guys showed up."

Everyone shared a look.

"There was a girl." Drake ran his hand through the top of his hair. "Ganna. Her name was Gabrianna, but she always used Ganna for short."

Ethan shivered. The fact that Drake was talking about Ganna in the past tense was not lost on him.

"Ganna was the second person to test the game when it was being developed." Drake frowned. "She was my best friend, so she naturally wanted to test the game with me. Nith was all too eager. After a few levels, Ganna found out I was trapped in here. That's when Nith confronted her. She fought hard, but in the end, she became the first soul collected in Nith's scepter. I haven't seen her since." Drake sighed and moved closer to the mirror. He stared deep inside as if he was watching the memory play out. "That's when I decided to make sure I was prepared." He held up his Guardian chain. "I knew Nith's scepter was the source of his power. I held the scepter and touched my chain. The chain lifted in the air and glowed. Then it landed back in my hand. A small wisp of purple vapor left the scepter, but it disappeared just as fast."

"So, is that like a weapon now?" Jason asked, pumping his fists in a boxer-like fashion. "Because I'm ready."

Drake shook his head. "It enhanced my chain. In my training sessions with Gordy, he taught me how to channel the power in the scepter. It was required in case Nith couldn't use it himself. Anyway, once you have the scepter, all you do is concentrate on what you need and it will be. In this case, I didn't want anything too obvious, otherwise it would tip Nith off. So I simply enhanced my Guardian Key—that is, this chain—to override any blockings in the security mirrors."

Alyssa eyed Drake's chain. "Why did you choose that? Couldn't you wish yourself out of here?"

Drake sucked in a deep breath. "No. I'm trapped here. I've been made part of the game. I can only leave when—or if—Nith loses his power." He turned to face Ethan and Brody. "Which is why I was relieved when Team Dynamite joined the game. Something about you gave me hope. And Nith must be scared of you if he took your sister so quickly. Usually he lets players get more addicted so they fight less when their souls are taken."

"S-souls," Ethan repeated. He had to get Maggie out of there. "We need to check on her! Now."

"I don't think you'll see anything different. But here it goes." He took his chain off. Then he walked closer to the mirror and touched the center of it with one hand. His other hand cradled the Guardian Key. "Show me Maggie."

The ripples in the mirror moved slowly. It was like watching water in a lake move on a calm, clear day after being touched by a soft breeze. Then they moved faster and faster until the ripples were clashing with each other. Finally, the tiny waves calmed and revealed a dark cell.

Once again, Maggie and Max were lying unconscious on the cement floor. This time there were many others with them. So. Many. People. Too many to count. All children.

They were all so . . . lifeless. Even—

"Maggie." Adrenaline rushed through Ethan's veins. His whole body shook so much that he felt he would never return to normal. He pounded on the mirror.

Jason grabbed Ethan's shoulders. "Yo, calm down. It'll be okay. We're Team Dynamite for a reason. We'll get her out of here. We'll get everyone out of here."

But it was as if Ethan didn't even hear Jason. All he could take in was Maggie in that cell. Then the image faded. "No." Ethan grabbed the mirror and tried to pull it off the wall, but it didn't budge. "Show me Maggie. Show me Maggie," he shouted, but the mirror remained dark. "Nooo." Ethan slumped down against the wall and held his head in his hands. "No, no, no." He could feel the tears burning his eyes, and he knew he was about to lose it.

All of his friends surrounded him.

"We have got to get her outta there," he sobbed. A chill ran through his heart. She disappeared because of his obsession with the game. Now she might be gone forever.

Alyssa sat on the floor next to him and patted his back. A tiny shred of warmth traveled through him at her touch, melting some of the coldness inside him. Her touch calmed his thoughts, and he made himself look up at her.

"We will," Alyssa assured him. "But we have to stay focused." She looked straight in his eyes. "Don't let Nith beat you. I know this is one of his games right now. He is toying with your emotions." Alyssa examined her nails, one by one. Ethan frowned. That was something Alyssa did when she tried to hide her nervousness.

"Maggie looked so still."

Drake stepped closer to Ethan and held out his hand. "Well, then, let's keep moving."

Everyone nodded.

Ethan wiped the tears from his eyes. They were right. Sobbing on the floor wouldn't help. The only sure way Maggie would stay trapped is if he stopped fighting. He wasn't going to let that happen. He owed it to her. He took Drake's hand and stood.

Drake and Jason led the way as Alyssa, Ethan, and Brody trailed behind. Several minutes of walking followed until they passed another security mirror. Ethan stopped.

"Oh, no." Alyssa grabbed Ethan's arm and Brody grabbed another. "Don't do it. All this will do is upset you."

Brody turned Ethan to face him. He stared at Ethan to hold his gaze. "C'mon. No more distractions, remember? We have to focus. If all we do is watch these mirrors, we'll never get out of here—or reach Maggie."

"Yea, you're ri—" Ethan started to say, but then another thought entered his mind. "Hey, Drake."

Drake stopped and turned around. He fidgeted with his chain, trying to get it back on.

"These mirrors work for everything, right?"

Drake gave him a confused look.

"I mean, they work like security cameras, don't they?"

Drake tilted his head. "Yeessss."

"Well, then, can't we use it to spy on Nith? And Gordy?"

Drake's eyes widened. "No. That is not a good idea."

Ugh, this is annoying, Ethan thought. *Why is Drake always afraid to make a move? We have to take risks if we want to help Maggie. And what could be so risky about checking a security mirror anyway?* He heard the rest of his friends talking, but he couldn't make the words out over his thoughts that blared in his head. It didn't matter anyway. He'd show them. He'd show them that he knew what he was doing.

Ethan couldn't explain what was happening inside him. His heart raced fast and he felt that familiar adrenaline rush through him. He ran up to Drake and grabbed the chain still lingering in his hands. He ran up to the mirror. "Show me Nith."

"No. Stop." It wasn't only Drake screaming. It was everyone. But it was too late. As the ripples gave way, Nith appeared in the mirror. He held his purple scepter and Gordy stood in front of it admiring it.

"Can I try? Can I try?" Gordy begged, jumping up and down.

"You fool. This is no toy," Nith roared, and he pushed Gordy to the ground. Gordy scrambled to his feet as Nith aimed the scepter at him. The purple ball glowed and Nith fired a shot to the side of Gordy, singeing the edge of his sleeve. "See?" Nith said.

At the same time, the chain in Ethan's hands glowed.

"In fact, it's—" Nith paused and spun around.

Ethan gulped. Did Nith know?

"Well, well, well." An evil smile curled across Nith's lips. "We aren't alone."

For a brief second, a twinge of panic flickered in Gordy's eyes.

He was probably fearing Nith's next round of punishments.

"It looks like our dear friend Ethan discovered our security mirrors."

CHAPTER 19 - The King's Chambers

Ethan's mouth dropped. How in the world did he know?

Alyssa glared at Ethan.

Nith stepped closer to his mirror. "You certainly have taken this game to a whole new level." Nith waved the scepter, and a computerized blueprint of the game lit up on the wall. Little yellow spots filled the blueprint, but the busiest parts were in the Grand Hall section and the beginning levels. "Many more have joined us."

Ethan turned his head. He couldn't look at it. He wanted to scream throughout the game to tell everyone to leave. He took a deep breath. He knew this was another Nith mind game. *Why didn't I listen to Drake?*

Drake ripped the chain out of Ethan's hand. "I tried to warn you. Nith's scepter picks up the signals when they are in a room where the mirror is activated, tipping him off to, you know, any spying."

Ethan didn't think Alyssa's glare could deepen, but it did, and she added a scowl for good measure.

Nith laughed. "Oh, calm down, Drake. It's not like anyone could really leave anyway. Nobody has even come close to the end of the game. Everyone who is trapped here is not going anywhere." He pointed to Ethan and his friends. "Even you."

With that, Nith waved his scepter again and vanished from the mirror.

"This isn't good." Jason gulped and looked at Brody, who nodded in agreement.

"We gotta move now," Drake insisted. "And no more stopping."

"Go?" Ethan stood in the same spot, not moving a muscle. "Go where? You heard him."

Drake nodded. "I did. But what he neglected to mention was that there is one way out of here. We have to find Nith and stop him . . . for good."

Ethan shuddered. It sounded so final. But if that's what it took to save his sister and Max, as well as anyone else stuck there, then that's what he'd do. "What do we have to do to stop him?"

Drake frowned. "It won't be easy. We must find him and then release the souls he trapped with his scepter. That will drain all his power." He took a deep breath. "The problem is, his power is growing by the second with more and more people being trapped in here. Everyone in here starts out walking the game, like we are. But as they encounter things—traps—they become stuck. That's when Nith 'harvests' their souls as a source for his magic."

Ethan nodded. "Then you're right. We better move. Now."

As they ran down the hall, it got darker and darker until Ethan could just make out the outline of his friends.

"Oh no, heads up," Drake called. Suddenly, the group came to a halt as a door blocked their path. Ethan realized too late and slammed into Drake, and then Jason and Alyssa crashed into him and Brody.

After everyone took a second to recover, Alyssa was the first to speak. "That's not a level door."

Brody approached the door and turned the knob. "It's not locked either."

Drake grinned and raised an eyebrow. "Yep. It's only a door."

They all followed Brody through the door and found themselves at the Grand Stairway in the Great Hall. The door they had come out of led directly to the set of steps facing the wall instead of the side they were on earlier. In fact, when they reached the top, there was no security mirror like there was on the other side. The marble bridges connected in the center where the steps stopped.

"Which way should we go?" Ethan asked.

"Judging from what I saw in the mirror," Drake said, eyeing Ethan, "I suggest we go right. It looked like he was in either the King's Bedroom or the Throne Room, both of which are this way."

The hallway had a black-and-white checkered floor. On the left side were marble banisters that reached Ethan's waist. When he looked over, he could see the entire Great Hall and all the arched doorways around the room. His eyes rested briefly on the Shadow Room and then the chamber. He frowned. Visiting those two rooms seemed like ages ago.

On Ethan's right, the walls were made of white smooth marble. There were three doorframes that Ethan could see, and they were outlined with intricate carvings. Tall pillars with deep grooves sandwiched each arched doorway. Smaller, evenly spaced arches bordered the tops of the wall and accented the doorways.

At least that's what Ethan thought they were. The doorways weren't wood or even metal. They were like windows draped with a thick veil of misty clouds.

Drake led them to the middle doorway.

Ethan swallowed hard as he approached the door. He looked at it and it felt like he was looking outside of a window of a building as tall as the sky. There was nothing under the clouds and there was nothing above them. There was only a vast landscape of . . . nothingness.

Ethan took a step forward with Brody, Alyssa, and Jason. Brody stuck his hand out as if reaching for the clouds. Drake held him back.

"It's another security measure. If you go through them, the clouds will devour you." He held out his Guardian of Bailiwick key. "I doubt this will work after the mirror incident with Nith—he had to have disabled my key by now—but here it goes."

He held his key on the left side of the doorway. A click sounded and the clouds vanished.

Jason pumped his fist in the air. "Awesome. We beat him to it."

Ethan swallowed hard. That was almost too easy. Drake caught his eye before continuing in. Alyssa moved up and walked with Ethan and Drake through the empty doorway and motioned for Brody and Jason to follow. As soon as they walked into the room, a majestic view greeted them. Across the room and centered against the wall was a large fireplace made of smooth white stone. A large gold box outlined with purple swirly details sat in the center on top. Across the front part of the mantle in Gothic-style lettering, the words *Bailiwick Fortress* were inscribed. Four logs sat perched in a pile, ready to feed the next fire. Stone gnome-shaped statues were on both sides of the fireplace. In fact, one looked eerily similar to the gnome from the maze earlier. A large king-sized bed lined the length of the wall to the left. Ethan should have guessed the canopy and sheets would be purple. Even the rug on the floor was purple. Everything about Nith involved purple. In the center of the room, a small round table and chairs sat in perfect form.

Alyssa made her way to the long couch across from the fireplace. She ran her fingers along the velvety material. "Everything looks so undisturbed—so perfect."

Jason turned toward the bed and smiled a mischievous grin. "How mad do you think Nith would be if I took a nap?" He positioned his hands over his head as if he were about to dive into a diving pool. Thankfully, Brody stopped him, though Ethan was pretty sure Jason wouldn't have done it. In a way, he liked how Jason used jokes to ease the anxiety of a situation.

Drake stared at the table in the center of the room. He walked over and picked something up. Were those earrings?

"What's that?" Alyssa asked.

"Hmm." Jason craned his neck toward Drake. "Looks like Nith likes dolphin earrings."

Drake put them in his pocket. "They're not his," he said with a grim expression. He turned to Jason. "They're Ganna's."

Shock and silence filled the room. Brody was the first to speak. He cleared his throat and pointed to each of the walls where there was an oval mirror similar to the one at the top of the grand stairs. "More mirrors. Why? Does he *always* have gamers searching his room?"

"Nope, you guys are definitely the first," Drake said. He moved closer to the mirror as if studying the ripples in glass.

Brody turned toward the door. "Well, Nith isn't in here."

"Yeah." Drake backed away from the mirror and joined Brody. "We should check the Throne Room before he—"

A loud click interrupted the group, and a look of horror crossed Drake's face. He rushed closer to the door. The cloudy veil returned, once again blocking the doorway. Drake held out his Guardian Key and touched the wall next to the door. Nothing. Whatever powers Drake once had in that key no longer applied. "Aaand never mind."

Just great, Ethan thought to himself. He was pretty sure they were trapped in the room now. Yet another thing keeping him from finding his sister.

"How are we going to get out of here now?" Alyssa kicked the leg of the couch.

Ethan looked around the room for anything they could use. The problem was he had no idea how to make a dangerous magical cloud door disappear. "Any other ideas, Drake?"

Drake opened his mouth to answer when a loud *swoosh* sounded in the fireplace. Ethan looked to see what the sound was. Flames enveloped the four wooden logs. Within seconds, the large fire consumed the entire fireplace, emanating waves of intense heat.

"We've got to find a way to disable that cloud door." Brody fanned himself as beads of sweat formed on his forehead.

Ethan scanned the room again. Maybe if he threw something through the clouds, it would consume the object and disable the veil. He grabbed one of the stone gnomes and tossed it through the cloudy door.

"What are you doing?" everyone asked at once.

Ethan watched as the clouds consumed the stone gnome. It tumbled and tumbled until he could no longer see it. There was never a crash or a thud, but he guessed there wouldn't be if the gnome was just "devoured" as Drake said would happen.

"Okay," Jason said, "*that* wasn't effective."

"You got a better idea?" Brody said in defense of Ethan. He stepped closer to Jason.

Jason frowned and turned away.

Alyssa patted Jason's arm. "There's definitely a way. There's got to be another way out. We just have to find it."

Ethan ran his fingers through his curly hair, which was damp from sweat. Was that fireplace getting hotter? "I really have no idea what other way out there could be, though." He wiped his damp hand on his jeans.

An uncomfortable silence filled the room. If everyone was thinking the same thing Ethan was, then they were as unsure as he was that they could find a way out.

The fire in the fireplace continued to grow. It looked like it was about to jump out of the fireplace. Ethan was so overheated that he thought he was hallucinating when he looked at the security mirror. The ripples in the glass grew and grew until an image of a room appeared. He squinted to make out the rest of the picture. As the ripples disappeared and the image gained focus, Ethan realized it was a view of the room where Maggie and the other Seeker prisoners were being held. She was still resting on Max, and both of them were asleep. However, the room was even more crowded than it was before. Rows and rows of people were packed in the room, covering every inch of the floor.

Ethan's heart raced and his body trembled. No matter how long he stared, he couldn't pull his gaze away. His little sister. All his fault. So. Many. People. He continued to stare. Faint voices reached his ears, but he couldn't make out what they were saying. Then, Ethan felt several hands on his arms. There was a pulling sensation, but he couldn't focus.

"Ethan..." Was that a female voice? It was so familiar.

"Ethan. Ethan." The voice grew louder. Alyssa?

He felt someone stand in front of him. He could feel their presence.

"ETHAN!" The voice was clear and loud now. He finally pulled his gaze from the mirror and looked at the person standing in front of him. Alyssa was there, still grabbing both of his arms. Tears streamed down her face. When her eyes met his, she took a deep breath. "Thank goodness."

"What happened?" Brody and Jason asked.

Ethan shivered. "I don't know. I saw Maggie and all those people in the security mirror and I couldn't pull myself away."

Drake shook his head. "There was nothing in the mirror." His eyebrows wrinkled. "Jason, Brody, and I tried to shake you out of it, but nothing. I've never seen the mirrors do something like that before." Drake tilted his head toward Alyssa. "It's a good thing she could reach you and pull you back."

"Yeah," Brody said. "That definitely felt like another Nith trick."

"Speaking of which." Jason pointed to the cloudy door. "We are still dealing with our previous Nith trick." He paused for a minute, then added, "Maybe there's a switch somewhere that will disable the veil."

Brody bit his lip. "I don't know. Drake already tried his key. That was probably the only way to do it."

Alyssa walked over to the fireplace, then immediately backed away from the out-of-control flames. "It won't hurt to look."

The group turned over every cushion, bedsheet, and rug. They moved every piece of furniture. They felt along every inch of the walls, and still they found nothing. Meanwhile, the fire continued to grow, and Ethan felt lightheaded.

"I don't think I can do this anymore," Ethan said and sat at the table, putting his head down on his arms. Sweat now poured off his forehead. He lifted his head. At least his friends didn't look any better—except maybe Alyssa. Drake's long hair was plastered against his neck. Brody's face was flushed. Jason's emo-styled hair was now loose and straggly, and he fanned himself with his hand. The heat affected Alyssa too, but while the rest of them looked a mess, she looked kinda cute. She pulled her long dark damp curls in a ponytail and rolled her sleeves up past her elbows.

And the fire. *The fire.* Ethan pulled himself out of his pondering and blinked hard. He couldn't be seeing this. The fire had grown and spilled out of the fireplace. It formed into a large ball and hovered over the floor. Then it stretched and pulled until it took the shape of a tall person—a tall fire-person—and it stared right at Ethan.

CHAPTER 20 - The Fiery Beast

Ethan jumped up out of his chair and leapt behind it for cover. It wasn't going to help, but he wasn't sure what would. How do you defeat a being made of fire?

The fire beast moved toward Ethan in slow, purposeful steps. Ethan expected everything that it touched to engulf in flames, but it only left ash in its path. It stopped several feet in front of him and held out its hand. A smaller ball of fire rested in its hand.

"Ohhhh, man," Jason said. "This can't be good."

"Everybody spread out." Brody held his arms out at both sides.

Everyone positioned themselves in a large circle around the being. It turned in circles trying to follow its targets. It let out a deep noise that sounded like something between a roar and a growl. With that, it threw the fireball at Ethan, who dodged to the side. The ball smashed into the wall but didn't go through it. Instead, it bounced off the wall and hovered in the air.

The creature held out its hand and turned it. Once its palm was facing up, the fireball returned to the center of the beast's palm as if it never left.

The beast continued to hurl the fireball repeatedly at the group. One came right at Drake, brushing his shoulder and knocking him to the ground. He screamed and clutched his arm. Brody and Jason ran over to him as the creature zeroed in on Drake, who scrambled backwards. It stalked closer to him and juggled the ball tauntingly.

Brody, Jason, and Alyssa stared with their jaws dropped. It was as if this thing was specifically after Drake. Brody quickly recovered and jumped in front of Drake. Ethan scanned the room quickly for something—anything—to stop the creature. He spotted another stone gnome and grabbed it. "Brody, Drake, move!"

Drake's eyes widened as Ethan lifted the gnome over his head, aiming for the center of his enemy. Drake scurried to his feet and dashed to the side with Brody right behind. Ethan hurled the statue. It collided with the creature but continued traveling through the fire. It sped out the other side and smashed into a wall. The gnome fractured into several charred pieces.

Ethan gulped. The fiery beast turned to him with vengeance in its flaming eyes.

"Okay," Jason said with a nervous laugh, "I think stone gnomes are on the 'doesn't work' list."

Brody, Alyssa, Drake, and Ethan nodded in agreement.

Another fireball whizzed past Ethan and then boomeranged back to the beast.

Drake tilted his head at Ethan. "What do you still have in your inventory?"

At first, Ethan had no idea what Drake was referring to. "My wha—oooooh." He waved his hand above his head, and the digital inventory of the tools he collected since starting the game appeared—several keys, the laser rings, the sword, the jugs of water. The water! There wasn't much. There were only two jugs, and it didn't look like enough to put out a huge personified fire, but maybe the others had some in their inventory. He reached for his jugs and tossed one to Brody. Everyone else did the same. Jason pulled out the ones he got from the dining room. When they distributed all the jugs, everyone had two.

"We have to make this count," Ethan said. "This is all we have, and we really shouldn't use it all at once." He turned to Jason with a grin. "But it's better than tossing stone gnomes at it."

Jason pointed at him. "Right? Exactly what I was saying!"

"Okay. Jason, Drake, and Alyssa, see if you can distract the fire-man-thingy."

The three friends spread out evenly in a half-circle in front of it. They each took turns taunting him. "Hey. Over here," Alyssa called to him. When it turned toward her, Drake yelled, "Yo, Fire-man. This way." It turned toward Drake. "Nah. Over here, you big, blazing lug," Jason called, positioning himself in a warrior yoga pose.

Brody opened his water jug and joined Ethan, who stood behind Fire-man. He crept as close as he could and considered the best place to throw the water. He tossed the contents of the jug at Fire-man's feet, hoping that would be the most effective move.

The fire sizzled and hissed, but that was all it did. Fire-man turned toward Ethan and Brody and stalked over to them. He got within inches of Ethan, but it was too close for Ethan to throw more water without getting hurt, so he nodded at Brody who already had his jug ready to go. Meanwhile, Drake, Alyssa, and Jason tossed their water at the creature as well.

"Guys, no." Ethan reached out to stop them, but it was too late. Worse, it did nothing to help extinguish the fiery creature.

They might as well have dumped the water in a sink for all

the good it did.

At the same time, Brody raced toward the beast but tripped over a chair. The jug launched out of his hand and toward Fire-man, but he swatted it away. The jug landed on the floor by the fireplace. Ethan snatched it up and unscrewed the top, fingers trembling. He had to make this count. It was their last water jug.

As Fire-man moved closer to him, Ethan fumbled with the water jug. He felt himself lose his grip of the container. "Noooo." Everything moved in slow motion. The jug tumbled out of his hands, slowly reaching for the ground until it banged against the iron gate of the fireplace. The water flew out of the jug, splashing the wood that was sitting inside.

Ethan kicked the chair. "That was our last water. What are we going to do now?"

They were out of options on making it out of the king's room. The thought of him never reaching his sister ripped a hole in his heart. How were they going to help anyone now?

Alyssa grabbed his arm. "Would you look!" She pointed to the fireplace. The wood sizzled where the water landed. He looked over at Fire-man, who was still there, but much smaller.

"How did throwing water on the logs do anything to shrink Fire-man?" Ethan asked.

Jason grinned. "I think you mean Fire-*boy*."

Ethan laughed. It definitely seemed less intimidating than it did a few moments ago.

Drake tossed his head to the side to move his long hair out of his face. "Those logs. Isn't that where the fire started?"

Everyone nodded.

"That was the source of the fire." Drake eyed Fire-boy. "That was no ordinary fire to begin with. Unfortunately, the water wasn't enough. Do we have anything to cover the logs? To smother out the rest of the fire?"

Jason tore off his sweater jacket. "This is all we have." He threw the jacket over the logs, and Fire-boy roared in protest. The smother of the fire on the logs started to shrink Fire-boy. He whirled fireball after fireball in every direction to stop it. Ethan and his friends dodged every one.

"He stopped shrinking," Brody said.

"I know," Ethan said. "We have to smother it more."

Alyssa untied the sweater she wore around her waist and tossed it on the fire.

Once again Fire-boy roared and hurled more fireballs. This time they were much smaller as Fire-boy shrunk even more. When he stopped shrinking, he was only two feet tall.

"Nothing's putting him out completely," Alyssa said. "We need something heavier."

Brody strode across the room to the bed and grabbed the purple blanket. "Maybe this will help. I have no doubt Nith is behind the fires. Maybe we need something from his world to defeat his monster."

Everyone nodded and Brody tossed the blanket over the remaining flames in the fireplace. Fire-boy let out a sound more like a yowl then a scream. He shrunk inch by inch, letting go of one more flimsy fireball before snuffing out completely.

Brody let out a heavy sigh.

"Now all we have to do is get past that cloudy door," Alyssa said, moving across the room to where the clouds still blocked their exit.

Drake walked over to the king's bed. "I know he has to have a switch in here somewhere for emergencies." He ran his hand behind the headboard and against the wall. "There's always more than one way for him to get around. He planned this carefully."

Ethan frowned. He was pretty sure Nith would not trap them in a room that they could easily escape from. "There's no way," he said.

Alyssa shook her head. "I disagree. It's the King's Bedroom. You seriously think there's no escape plan?"

Brody nodded. "Yeah. I mean, I bet that's why Nith sent us Fire-man."

The conversation continued for a few minutes with everyone going back and forth.

"There it is." A loud click sounded behind a painting by the bed, stopping the conversation in its tracks. "Quick." Drake ushered everyone out of the room. "It will only disable the clouds for a few seconds."

Everyone was almost out of the room when Alyssa stopped and turned back into the room.

"What are you doing?" Ethan ran and grabbed her arm. "We gotta go. Now!"

Alyssa snatched her arm back. "My ring!" She dropped to the floor and ran her fingers across the floor. "I lost my ring."

"How did you lose your—" Jason started.

"I put it in my pocket for safekeeping. I'm not leaving without it," Alyssa said.

The cloudy veil formed around the edges of the doorway, slowly creeping toward the center. Alyssa glanced around the room, and her sweater resting in the fireplace caught her eye. She rushed over and pulled out what was left of it. She shook it as a cloud of ash swarmed around her.

Ethan eyed the clouds. The veil was about halfway complete. "Alyssa, just leave it," he called as she shook the sweater again.

"Nope. I got it," Alyssa yelled as the ring fell to the floor. She quickly snatched it up. She and Ethan raced for the door and made it through just before the cloudy veil reappeared in the doorway.

CHAPTER 21 - The Throne Room

Ethan glanced at Alyssa as the group ventured further down the hallway. She gently placed her ring back on her pointer finger and rested her hand over it. Nobody uttered a word, but Ethan wondered if they were thinking the same thing he was. They'd battled dragons, rooms, gnomes, mazes, fires, and monsters, but they still had yet to get what they came for: freeing Maggie and Max, not to mention anyone else who was trapped there. Ethan wondered how many more people were trapped in Seeker. Every time the security mirrors activated, it seemed that there were double—if not more—the people he had seen before. It felt like all Nith was doing was playing games, making them run in circles. Each time they left a room, they succeeded, but he still felt no closer to getting to Maggie than he did earlier.

Drake stopped halfway down the marble hallway. "Since Nith was not in the king's chambers, he had to have been in the Throne Room."

Brody folded his arms. "You know we probably won't be able to get in, right? Since your Guardian Key is disabled, you have about as much access as we do."

Jason nodded in agreement.

Drake pushed his hair out of his eyes. "We'll find a way in if we have to. I have a feeling he'll be waiting for us."

Drake turned back and faced the path in front of them. Alyssa and Ethan joined him as Brody and Jason walked behind them.

When they arrived at the end of the hallway, Drake walked up and stopped right in front of a picture hanging on the wall. It was an oil painting of Nith, sitting in a golden throne and holding his scepter. The glowing purple orb on top of the scepter was meager compared to when Ethan first met Nith in the Shadow Room. In the picture, Gordy the gnome stood to the right and Drake stood to the left. Drake frowned at the picture. Then he took a deep breath and lifted it. Drake pressed his key firmly against the wall where the picture was. Nothing happened.

"Isn't your key disabled?" Brody asked.

Drake nodded. "Yes, but it couldn't hurt to try. Not sure how we'll get in."

Ethan thought about his sword and how it had been helping them get through tough situations. It seemed to have power behind it. "Let me try something," Ethan said. He opened his inventory and pulled out the sword. He held it in front of the picture. It glowed in response. Lifting it up in the air, it twisted until it morphed into a key.

Drake grinned. "You're catching on to the tricks of this place."

Ethan nodded. "Was worth a shot."

"That's my man," Jason said, throwing his arm over Ethan's shoulders. "Always thinking."

Ethan grinned and placed the key against the wall where Drake had tried before. This time, the picture wobbled and then pushed in as if it were a button. The wall to the right slid up and revealed another long passageway.

Drake smiled and motioned to Ethan and his friends.

"This way."

They slowly followed the aisle, which was a continuation of the hall. Eventually, the black-and-white checkered floor gave way to a smooth stone path.

After walking for several minutes in silence, they finally came to a double doorway outlined with gold borders. Subtle designs were illustrated on the door with gold. There were symbols of game controllers, Nith's scepter, and children. There was an image of the Transport, which next to Nith was the second-largest image on there. Next to the doors was another picture. This one was of Nith standing in his Throne Room holding his scepter by his side like a staff. Drake lifted the picture and pressed a purple button on the wall, which opened the doors in front of them.

Drake looked at everyone directly. "Ready for this?"

Everyone nodded.

Ethan took a deep breath and nodded as well. He wasn't sure what was going to happen or how he was going to handle it, but he knew one thing: Nith *would* give him his sister back. Ethan would make sure of it.

They stepped forward into the large, vast room. A giant purple area rug covered the majority of the oval room. There were small wooden tables on the room's two side walls. Straight across was a small set of stairs that had about four steps to them. On the top, a spacious marble platform sat with only a solitary throne. Its purple cushions matched the area rug below.

Jason squatted down and touched the rug. "I had a feeling that whatever was in here was going to be purple."

Alyssa laughed. "Ya don't say."

Brody grinned. "Hmm. What gave you that idea?"

A spark of irritation surfaced in Ethan, but he took a deep breath and ignored the conversation. He couldn't explain why it bothered him so much when Alyssa enjoyed Jason's jokes. Instead, he returned his focus back to the throne ahead of them. Something about the single throne looked lonely to Ethan. He wondered if Nith chose this world—*created* this world—like that on purpose. After all, it was his creation, so he could design it any way he wanted. And yet he chose to rule completely alone aside from having Drake and Gordy under him. Ethan shuddered at the thought. He couldn't imagine living—especially forever—without his family and friends.

A deep voice that could only be Nith's interrupted Ethan's thoughts. "So glad you all could join me on this special occasion." His voice came from across the room, and he was not alone. Gordy was with him as well as a girl.

"Oh great." Jason threw his hands up over his head. "You again."

Nith clicked his tongue. "You were looking for me, were you not?"

"Yeah, well, I was hoping it'd take a little longer," Jason shot back. "Nice fire trick, by the way."

"I'm glad you liked it," he sneered, turning his attention to Drake. "Though it was meant for you to enjoy."

Drake stepped in front of Ethan and Jason and nodded his head toward Nith. "Not really my thing."

Nith stalked halfway across the room toward the group, dragging the girl with him. "I'm pretty sure she is your 'thing,' Drake." His long dark hair was tucked inside his hooded cape. The girl had beautiful light-brown hair that reached the middle of her back. Her long bangs rested above her tiny eyes. She was pretty, but she had a dismal look to her.

Her eyes looked sunken and seemed . . . blank.

Drake sucked in a breath. He reached out a shaking hand and then brought it back to his side. "G-Gabrianna," he whispered. He shook his head as if shaking the thought away. "It can't be." He stepped closer. Nith held out his hand to stop him. Drake studied her. "It is you, Ganna. But how?"

He reached out to her, but Nith yanked her back. Gordy stood in front of them, blocking Drake's access.

"You." Drake pointed above Gordy and at Nith. "Keep your hands off her." He turned back to Ganna. "Are you okay? Ganna?"

Nith pulled her closer to him. "Gabrianna—or Ganna, as you two seem to go with—has awoken." He stared at Drake. It was so cold, even Ethan could feel it pierce through him. "I released her soul from here." He twirled his scepter. "I decided to make her my new Guardian of Bailiwick."

"No." Drake pushed past Gordy and moved closer to Ganna. He bent his head down to look into her eyes. "You don't have to do this. Don't let him do this to you."

Ethan's heart sank. He could almost feel the fear and helplessness radiate from Drake. Ethan had never seen Drake like that. He couldn't look anymore and turned his gaze on Gordy, who shifted uncomfortably.

Nith threw his head back and laughed. "Too late, my friend. She *is* the new Guardian." He turned to the group and sneered. "I've known Drake long enough to expect he'd betray me eventually, which is why I kept her away from the other souls I trapped here. Oh, don't look at me like that." Nith pointed to Drake whose scowl could scare the bravest of the brave. "She's perfectly safe. She even rested in the king's room until I was ready. Now that she's Guardian, the next step to my plan has begun." He turned to Gordy and motioned for him to approach.

Alyssa stepped up next to Drake and addressed Ganna. "Come with us. We can help you." She looked directly into Ganna's eyes. "Drake's right. You don't have to do this."

Something flickered in Ganna's eyes before she turned away.

"Oh, but she does," Nith answered for Ganna. "She knows that when my plan is complete, our worlds will merge, and she will rule alongside me." He turned to Ganna and glared. "She also knows it is her—and Drake's—only chance of survival. Isn't that right?"

Ganna stood and stared, not saying anything, but tears formed in the corner of her eyes. Ethan eyed Drake, who sat fixated on Ganna. Jason and Brody moved next to Alyssa. Ethan joined them, and Drake was surrounded by his friends and their support.

Gordy stood as still as a statue—except for his eyes, which darted between Drake, Ganna, and Ethan.

"You still have a choice." Brody held out his hand for Ganna to take. Her eyes flashed to Drake, pleadingly, but she didn't move. Brody moved forward to take her arm.

"Ah-ah-ahhh," Nith chided and pointed his scepter right at Ganna. "I wouldn't interfere."

Drake jumped in front of Brody, blocking any access Brody had to Ganna.

Nith smiled. "Wise decision. Now, the key, Gabrianna," Nith ordered.

She gulped, then moved closer to Drake, stopping inches away from him. She slowly reached out, holding her hand out with her palm facing up, still saying nothing.

"No," Drake said. He stood with his feet firmly planted on

the ground. "You will have to take it from me. I know you don't want to do this."

She turned her head and looked away. After several seconds, she took a deep breath and reached for Drake. She slipped both hands behind his neck, pushing his long hair to the side. She unclasped the chain, then brought one hand to his cheek. Her hand rested there for a minute and their eyes met before she brought her hands together with the chain inside. She stared at her hands, then looked into Drake's eyes again. Neither one said a word, but it felt like so much was said between them. Then, she turned around and walked back to Nith. She handed him the chain, and he placed the Guardian Key around her neck. Ganna bowed her head as Nith touched the key with the scepter. A small purple light sparked. The key lifted slightly in the air, glowed, then rested back on her neck as Nith returned all access that had recently been revoked.

"We're ready now," Nith said to Gordy, who jumped forward and grabbed Ganna's arm.

"Ready for what, exactly?" Alyssa asked, folding her arms across her chest.

"I doubt that he will tell us anything," Brody said evenly.

"It's not like he's the brightest gnome in Seeker," Alyssa said, moving her hands to her hips. "So what's going on, gnome? Or can't you handle telling us?"

Gordy's face turned an angry shade of red. "You have no idea who you're talking about, Alyssa," Gordy sneered. "I happen to be—" Nith stared hard at Gordy. "About ready to leave," Gordy finished. Then Nith pointed to Gordy, who greedily snapped his fingers. A thick purple fog filled the room, and when it cleared, Gordy, Nith, and Ganna were gone.

CHAPTER 22 - Ronald

Drake hung his head and slid to the floor. He pulled his knees to his chest and rested his head on top. His hair surrounded his face, and Ethan was pretty sure it was hiding Drake's tears.

"I lost her . . . again," Drake said. His voice sounded far away. He shook his head. "I swore if I ever saw her again, I wouldn't let this happen a second time." He looked around the room. "But here we are."

Brody and Jason sat down next to Drake.

"We'll get her back," Brody said.

Jason nodded. "Seriously. We're out here to help Maggie." He looked directly at Ethan when he said that. "And Max . . . oh, and every other trapped gamer here." He grinned. "Getting Ganna out will be a piece of cake."

Alyssa held her hand out to Drake. "C'mon. We're Team Dynamite. We can't give up now."

Ethan also offered his hand to Drake, along with Brody and Jason. Drake reached up with both hands and, with the help of the group, pulled himself up off the floor. "You're right. She's okay. She might be under his control, but she is okay. There's a chance we can still help her."

Jason turned serious. "We *will* help her."

Everyone nodded, including Ethan. Drake and Alyssa were right. They were a team. No matter what. And the same way Drake shouldn't let his despair over Ganna get in the way, Ethan knew he shouldn't let his frustration—or jealousy?—get in the way of their goal either. If only it wasn't so hard.

"Where do you think they disappeared to?" Ethan asked Drake as they exited the Throne Room on the other side. It led them to a thin hallway surrounded by thick glass walls. Ahead of them was a tall tower.

Drake pulled his leather jacket closer to his body. "I'm betting they're heading to The Keep at the top of that tower. It sounded like they're about to do something big." He pointed to the tall building in front of them.

"What's so important about The Keep?" Alyssa asked.

Jason pointed to the highest points of the tower, which looked like rectangular stalls surrounding the edges of the top of the building. "I bet he can see everything from there. What better place to do something drastic and Nith-like?"

The group continued in silence. Ethan had a feeling everyone was wondering the same thing Ethan was: how were they possibly going to stop Nith?

Finally, Brody interrupted the silence. "So what's the story with Ganna? She's obviously important to you."

Drake nodded and ran his fingers through his hair. "Yeah. We grew up together and were inseparable. My uncle was a great computer programmer who was always trying to develop 'the next big thing' in gaming. He had me and Ganna come over all the time to give him insight on gaming trends and what kids liked to play."

Ethan gave Brody a look. Drake's uncle was a programmer? That was . . . interesting.

At last, Drake found the rest of the words he was looking for. "Do you know how I was the first person in this game?"

Alyssa walked over and stood next to Ethan. She eyed Drake suspiciously. "No. You're making me nervous." She glanced at Ethan as he gulped. She pointed to him and said, "You're making *him* nervous."

Drake sighed. He stared at his feet, and his long hair hung around his face. He looked up at them and moved his mouth to form words, but nothing came out. He cleared his throat a few times before finally managing to activate his voice.

"My uncle, Ronald Tinim, lived for gaming. He would eat, drink, and sleep gaming. He even studied video game design and created some of his own games. After playing for years with his best friend, they decided to enter a gaming competition. They practiced every day. When the competition was only a week away, Uncle Ronald noticed something with the game's algorithm. He wrote down several pages of notes. Over the course of the week, he continued to practice with Aiden. Then, one day, Uncle Ron's notes were missing. He searched the entire house, ripping everything in the gaming room apart, but he couldn't find them."

"Okay, but what—" Brody asked, but Drake held up his finger.

Alyssa shook her head and whispered to Ethan. "Ronald Tinim." She was so close to him that he could feel her breath on his cheek. "Why does that sound familiar?"

Ethan looked at Alyssa. Now that she mentioned it, he had heard that name somewhere.

Drake shuffled his feet but refused to look at anyone. "Anyway, the day of the competition came. Uncle Ron used whatever information he could remember from his notes to play the game. There were hundreds of competitors. After several rounds, the pool was down to five players. Uncle Ron and Aiden were two of the five. Then the game was down to two people, Uncle Ron and his best friend. It was then that Uncle Ron realized what may have happened to his notes. They battled each other for an hour before Aiden took over and won the game. Uncle Ron noticed the winning action was one of the tricks he had written in his notes."

Alyssa looked at Ethan. "Which means his best friend cheated Ronald out of his win."

"Exactly," Drake said. "Uncle Ron was furious. He started freaking out, yelling and screaming at Aiden in front of everyone, slamming his fist in his gaming booth. Security had to kick him out of the building, and he was banned from ever competing there again."

"Wow, rage much?" Jason asked.

Drake nodded. "He took his games seriously. Unfortunately for him, so did the competition organizers. They had strict sportsmanship rules. He broke them and had to pay the consequences. After that, his girlfriend broke up with him. Apparently, his rage scared her. Aiden also disappeared from his life."

Brody, who had been leaning against one of the glass walls, pushed himself off with his foot. "Did Aiden and his girlfriend—"

Drake shrugged. "I don't know for sure, but Uncle Ron always grumbled that Aiden not only stole his notes but his girlfriend, too. In one day, he lost everything."

"What did your uncle do about it?" Brody asked.

Jason held out his hand. "I'm going to go out on a limb here and guess that 'Uncle Ron' didn't handle it too well."

Drake shook his head and laughed a bitter laugh. "You got

that right. In the beginning, everything was fine. He decided to create his own game." He stopped there and looked at everyone. Alyssa's mouth dropped open. Brody, Jason, and Ethan all exchanged looks.

"As long as I could remember, he was always working on his 'masterpiece,'" Drake said. "As I told you before, he studied game design and played around with creating some."

Drake let out a long, slow breath before continuing. "He wanted to be someone. To be known. He could no longer compete in competitions, so he decided he would create the best gaming company ever and create the best gaming experience ever. He experimented with what would happen if he could create a game that felt like the player was really there. He wanted it to be as real of an experience as he could make it."

Ethan froze. "You mean like what would happen if we used things like, say, special headsets?"

"Or in a game that makes it possible to see, hear, and interact as we do outside the game?" Alyssa added.

Drake nodded. "Remember the tiny prickle you felt when you first put on the Transport? There's a reason for that. It's connecting with your brain. And the name Tinim probably sounds familiar to you, because that is the company name that founded Seeker."

Everyone stared at him in shock. Ethan remembered when he first opened the Transport and read the label. Ethan grabbed Drake's arm and spun him around. This sounded like pretty important information, and once again, Drake held out on them. His heart pounded as he questioned Drake. "Did you ever plan on mentioning this to us?" He felt his face flush and his heart now felt like it was thumping out of his chest. "Or is it fun for you to watch us slowly—and I mean *slowly*—figure things out?"

Alyssa placed a hand on Ethan's arm. He turned and looked at her. She raised her eyebrows when their eyes met and gave him her "keep calm and get the info" look. He took a deep breath. Alyssa was right. Alienating Drake would not help them in any way.

"That's not all." Drake walked up to a security mirror in the hallway and ran his fingers down the mirror's frame. He waved his arms around. "All of this is my uncle's design. He created it all."

"Where's your uncle now?" Ethan asked. "In some fancy office while my sister and friends are trapped in here?"

Drake shook his head. "I don't know. The day I went over to test the game, something went wrong with the headset. Before I knew it, I was literally transported into the game. That was the last I ever saw of Uncle Ron."

Jason let out a long, low whistle. "He hasn't come looking for you?"

Drake shook his head.

"Maybe he got sucked in as well," Jason added. "Do you think he's trapped here too?"

"He can't be," Alyssa said. "The game has been released and is super popular, so he has to be out there selling the game."

"True," Drake said, "but he already sold the game to distributors. We were testing the equipment one more time before everything went live."

Ethan's stomach soured. If that was true, Ronald Tinim might have gotten stuck in the game too. He turned to Drake. "Do you think Nith is Ronald?"

Drake shook his head. "Impossible. Nith was already a

character in the game before I was trapped here."

Ethan nodded. "Makes sense. We'll keep an eye out for him. I'm sure he's trapped here somewhere too."

CHAPTER 23 - The Keep

"C'mon," Ethan said as he headed toward the tower. "Every second we are stopped we are allowing Nith and Gordy to get further ahead of us."

They made their way down the glass-enclosed pathway, which led them out of the main fortress and through the courtyard.

Ethan, who was several feet ahead of them walking with Alyssa, pointed to The Keep ahead. "Looks like we're almost there."

"Yeah. The entrance should be lined up with this path." Drake jogged to catch up to Ethan. "We've conquered several rooms in the fortress, but The Keep is the most secure." He looked directly at Ethan. "So be ready for a challenge."

Ethan grinned. "Always."

Alyssa smiled at him. "Let's do this?"

He tilted his head toward her. "Yeah, let's do this."

Drake and Ethan led the rest of the group down the remainder of the path. They stopped when they approached the arched entrance to the circular building. It had a gold plaque with the words "Bailiwick Keep" on it. From the distance, Ethan thought The Keep was made of grey stone, like the many he had seen before in books. But now that he was closer, he realized the grey was actually a grey-and-white marble texture that stretched from the bottom of the building all the way to the top. Tall thin columns extended above the top floor and spaced evenly around the highest level of the building. A stone carving of Nith and his scepter sat on a crest in the center of the doorway.

"How are we going to get in?" Brody asked.

"We should try your keys," Drake said, pointing at Ethan.

"What keys?" Jason asked with his hands on his hips.

"The inventory." Alyssa waved her hand in the air and the digital inventory appeared. The spot with Team Dynamite's keys lit up. She reached for the keys. "Does it matter which one?"

"Probably not," Drake said. "We need a golden key to swipe over the statue on the door."

Jason reached up and touched the stone carving of Nith. He looked at Ethan and grinned. "Is he talking about this ridiculous door statue of the crazy wizard and his toy?"

"The scepter is no toy." Drake shook his head. "The source of the purple power coming from his scepter is the emotions and energy—the soul—of every unconscious player trapped inside the game."

Ethan's eyes widened. "You–you mean my sister is probably trapped in there?"

Drake sighed. "Not physically. Though she is unconscious with the others, everyone is still in the holding room we saw in the security mirror."

Ethan took a step back. "But her soul—or at least part of it—could be in there."

Drake lowered his head and said nothing. That was all the answer Ethan needed. This power-hungry monster, for whatever reason, was playing not only with people's lives, he was toying with their souls. When Alyssa looked at Ethan, he could see the concern in her eyes. He quickly looked away, blinking back tears.

Alyssa took the first golden key out of the inventory and swiped it in front of the statue. A light above it blinked blue and then red. After that, nothing happened.

Alyssa looked at Drake.

Drake scratched his head. "I don't understand. That's usually all we need."

Brody stepped up. "Well, if all we need are the golden keys to get in here, The Keep wouldn't be as secure as you said it was earlier."

Drake looked closer at the statue, checking each side of it and the area where the light was. He stepped back, still eyeing the statue. "Not many people get past the first level of the fortress. Since we got through the second level, there should be nothing to stop the keys from working. The more keys you have, the more power behind them."

Jason waved his hand in the air and grabbed another key. "Let's let a pro try." He took the key and strode over to the statue with his head held high. He swiped his key in front of the statue. He held his arms out, pointing to the statue as if to say "ta-da." The light blinked blue. There was a pause that seemed to last forever, and then it blinked . . . red. Jason slapped his hands at his side. "Aww, c'mon."

"Nith is definitely in there," Ethan said. He had to be if he was trying to keep them out so badly. "He probably switched the activation key. He knows Drake knows to use the golden keys." Brody opened his inventory and scanned it. "I bet Nith glitched the inventories to disable the keys we earned from all the levels. What else can we use? There are the laser rings and the sword."

Ethan rested a finger above his lip as he ran the possibilities through his head. Was there something they were missing from the inventory? He couldn't see using a laser ring to get through. What were they going to do? Shoot at it? And the sword. What would a sword have to do with The Keep?

"Isn't The Keep typically a way to defend the rest of the castle from attackers?" Ethan asked.

Drake nodded slowly and he met Ethan's eyes. "You think the sword is the 'key' to The Keep."

Ethan grinned. "And come to think of it, didn't it turn into a key when we left the maze?" He waved his hand in the air. "Plus, I have a feeling not many people come across the sword. I happened to get one during my battle in the maze."

He reached up and pulled the sword down. The hull glowed for a second, then returned to normal. He held it with both hands in front of him and stepped closer to the door until he was inches from the statue. He waved it in a semicircle in front. The sword grew warm and glowed. It elevated in the air and transformed into a key. Ethan grabbed the key and swiped it by the statue. The light blinked blue . . . blue . . . then finally . . . green. Instantly there was a click and the door swung open.

Jason rushed in ahead of them. He was already in the center of the room by the time everyone got inside. "Yooo. Look at this place."

Ethan moved in beside him and looked around. The Keep was two stories high. The bottom level had marble walls that reached up to the balcony, which separated the bottom level from the top level. At the top of the walls on the lower level, purple fabric was draped in even increments along the perimeter of the room. In between each divot was a gold tassel with a mini golden key attached to the front. In the center of each wall was one oval security mirror. Several decorative armored shields sat towards the walls by the entrance, and beautiful shiny metal knights stood in each corner of the room. The floor was made of oak panels, which matched the oak steps resting against the back wall.

The group climbed the steps, which led to an iron balcony lining the walls of the upper level. Ethan walked along the balcony and stopped halfway across. He looked over the balcony to the lower level. He could see the entire room except for the area directly under him.

He turned back to his friends as they crossed the room and reached the right-hand corner of the upper level. A purple curtain, covered in the same golden decorations as the fabric below them, hung loosely in the corner. Ethan pushed it aside to reveal a steep spiral staircase.

Nobody said a word as they glanced at each other. Then, one by one since there was only enough room for one person on a step, they stepped onto the metal staircase. Ethan grabbed both railings as he climbed, climbed, climbed his way up. Brody followed behind, followed by Jason, Alyssa, and then Drake.

Ethan cringed as echoes rang out with each step they took. If Nith was up there, they were definitely ruining the element of surprise. Jason's steps seemed louder than everyone else's. Every step was a thump, thump, thump. "I'm seriously ready to hurl these boots over the railing," Jason hissed.

They continued climbing higher and higher. Ethan's legs were starting to burn and felt heavier with each step. They must have been getting close because the steps were getting narrower and smaller. Finally, he reached the top. He moved through the doorway onto an elevated stone path that circled the outside of The Keep. A purple flag embroidered with the words *Fortress of Bailiwick* in gold lettering sat fastened to one of the four marble walls. The crest on the flag was of Nith, holding his scepter, surrounded by images of the Transport and the Seeker logo. To the left was a perfectly shining metal knight standing in a guarding position, adding a perfect accent to the area.

Other than the knight and the flag, there was nothing else that caught his attention.

"Looks like this was a bust," Jason said and made his way to the steps.

Alyssa walked to one of the lookouts. She rested her hands on the wall as she looked over it. Ethan smiled as Alyssa's hair blew lightly in the breeze. For that one minute, everything seemed calm and normal. He felt his heart flutter when she turned her head over her shoulder and looked at him. She motioned for him to come over. When he joined her, she pointed to the ground below. Whatever warm and fuzzy feelings he experienced a few seconds before vanished at what came next. There were hundreds of people outside The Keep. They surrounded the building, moving in slow steps, and they were headed straight for them.

CHAPTER 24 - Temptations

"Where did they all come from?" Brody peered over the edge. The massive crowd was closing in on the building.

"Max!" Brody pointed to a boy in the crowd. "I think I see Max there!"

Drake rushed to the wall and joined Brody. His face drained of color. "They aren't just people. They're the players."

"Well, yeah, we figured that," Jason said. "Isn't everyone in here playing the game?"

Drake shook his head. "No. I mean they're all the ones we saw in the security mirror trapped in the holding room."

A glimmer of hope ran through Ethan. Could that mean Maggie . . . "Are they free? Did they somehow escape?"

Drake flipped his hair out of his eyes. "No. Look at them."

Ethan couldn't bring himself to do it—he was filled with too much hope—but Alyssa grabbed his hand and pointed over the wall. For a minute, everything seemed okay as her hand covered his. He gathered up the courage and looked over the edge. As long as her hand was there, he could face anything.

The people were all walking, but it was as if something was pulling them forward. There was no emotion on their faces or fluid movement with their steps. It was almost as if they were sleepwalking. Leading the group was Gordy, and directly behind him was a blonde girl who looked exactly like . . .

"Maggie," Ethan screamed. "Maggie."

"Shhh." Drake pulled Ethan back from the wall and ducked. He motioned for everyone to get down. "She won't hear you, but Gordy might."

"Well, I can't just stand here."

Brody walked over and rested his hand on Ethan's shoulder. "We're not. We're going to do something . . . right?" He stared hard at Drake.

"Right," Alyssa answered before Drake could say anything.

"Right," Jason added.

Drake sighed. "You don't think I tried fighting back? You think I voluntarily stayed here as a part of Nith's sick world? Those people"—he pointed over the wall—"are under his control. They aren't players anymore. Your sister is not herself anymore. This is an army Nith created in case someone chose to fight back. We have, and now they're coming after us."

"Well, then," Alyssa said, "it looks like we're on to something if Nith's army is coming after us, don't you think?"

"That may be true." Drake ran his hand through his hair. "But Nith is powerful. Look how many people he has under his control. Look how many souls he has collected."

As if illustrating his point, a sea of people surrounded The Keep.

"Well, we have to try. That's my sister in there." Ethan paused when his voice cracked. Then he added, "I owe it to her to be there for her. I wasn't there before. She's counting on me to come through. And I will. Even if I have to do it alone."

With that, he rushed to the metal staircase and flew down the steps. He didn't hear any footsteps echoing behind him, but he didn't care. He was going to get to Maggie and get her out of there. When he reached the upper level of the tower, he flew across the room to the next stairway and raced down. He didn't stop to look behind him. Down, down, down he went, two steps at a time. When he reached the bottom level, heaving to catch his breath, the sea of people from outside poured through the doorway.

Ethan braced himself for a confrontation, but they all ignored him. They walked along the right wall and stopped at a door in the back of the room. He wasn't even sure if they were awake. Their eyes were open, but they didn't respond to anyone or anything. When they could no longer move forward, they slid to the floor and sat, holding their knees to their chest.

Well, that was easy, he thought.

Maggie was still standing with Gordy, who led her to the front and center of the group of people. All of them faced Ethan, staring blankly at him. Even Maggie. The only one who showed any emotion was Gordy, who wore a glare.

"There you are!" Alyssa was the first to reach Ethan.

Jason was right behind her. He rested his hand on Alyssa's shoulder, but the rest of him was doubled over. "You are one fast dude," he said in between breaths. Finally, he stood up straight, but his hand still sat on Alyssa's shoulder. Ethan stared at Jason's hand as Brody and Drake made it down the stairs. Brody followed Ethan's gaze. "Everything alright here?"

Jason removed his hand and spun to face Brody. "Yeah. Had to catch my breath after chasing that one." He pointed to Ethan.

"What are they doing?" Brody pointed to the stream of people at the back door and along the wall.

"There's a huge dungeon through that door." Drake nodded to the back door. "My guess is—"

A thunderous boom echoed, followed by a plume of purple smoke coming from the center of the room. "Well, we meet yet again," Nith said. "Not ready to give up, I see."

Ethan glared at Nith, who stood with Ganna. There were glowing purple handcuffs connecting Ganna's left wrist with a metal latch on Nith's cloak. Gordy strode up and stood on Nith's other side. Nith's scepter rested in his right hand. The glowing purple orb was the size of a watermelon now, and Ethan remembered Nith's words from before: *"Every time someone permanently joins our world, my power source grows."* The terrifying thought made him shiver.

Nith turned his eyes on Ethan. "You still have time to reconsider my offer. Join us—" he waved to Ganna and Gordy and then to the crowd of people with his scepter "—and everyone you care about will be freed."

Ethan crinkled his eyebrows. *Why would Nith do that?*

"You have great energy, Ethan. When you let the rush from your anger—" he looked at Jason "—or jealousy—" he looked at Alyssa "—run free, you can accomplish many things. When you join me, you not only guarantee sweet Maggie's safety, but you will also gain something more: power."

Drake nudged Ethan. "No deals," he hissed.

Nith responded by aiming his scepter at Drake's foot. A purple bolt of lightning struck his boot, leaving a pin-sized hole. The force knocked Drake backwards and to the ground. "Enough from you, traitor."

But Drake was right. Nith could not be trusted. As much as Ethan wanted to guarantee Maggie's freedom, he was pretty sure taking this deal would mean the complete opposite.

"You should take the deal," Gordy said. "You have no idea what you are up against."

"We'll take our chances," Brody said.

"Yeah, no offense," Jason said, "but you aren't the most reliable source here . . . or the smartest!"

Gordy gritted his teeth but said nothing. Instead, he turned to Nith. "I told you this was a waste of time."

Nith narrowed his eyes. "You are in no position to tell me anything." He turned his attention back to Ethan.

Gordy glared at Nith. "You know I'm getting really sick and—"

Nith aimed his scepter at Gordy.

"Never mind," Gordy said in a hurried and shrieky voice.

Brody held out his hand and pointed to Gordy. "Is *that* the kind of power you want?" He stood in front of Ethan. "If that's what he'd do to Gordy, imagine what he'd do to you." He waved his arm at the rest of the group. "Or to the rest of us."

Nith turned back to Ethan. "The time is drawing near. I'm about to merge the digital world with your world. It will be so much better—we will have the best of both worlds combined into one. You can either join us now and be part of the digital royalty or you can refuse, condemning yourself, your friends, and your sister to slavery." Nith examined his fingers as if that was the most important thing occurring now. He looked back at Ethan. "Your choice."

It sounded so tempting. Maggie would be safe. That's what he came for. That is what he wanted. And he'd have power in the new world Nith was creating. An added bonus—Alyssa would see that the power to keep them all safe was more appealing than Jason's goofy humor.

Ethan's eyes widened and his breath caught. Guilt immediately crept through him. *How could I even think those things? And about my friends? Was I really considering selling my soul to that thing?* He lifted his head and eyed Nith. Ethan knew he was better than that.

"Everything involving you has been a lie or a trick," Brody shouted. "You think he's going to trust you now?"

"Yeah, in case you haven't noticed, Ethan is a little bit smarter than that," Alyssa said with a glare. She turned and looked at Ethan hopefully.

Brody stood tall next to Ethan. "Yep, definitely not born yesterday."

"Oh, we're quite aware of that, aren't we, Gordy?" Nith sent him a crooked smile.

Gordy rolled his eyes. "Real clever. Let's focus on the issue at hand, shall we?" He locked eyes with Ethan. "Are you in or out?"

Drake's eyes narrowed at Gordy, and for the next several minutes, he didn't take his eyes off him. *What is going through Drake's mind?* Ethan wondered.

But Ethan couldn't worry about that now. The fact that Nith and Gordy kept pushing Ethan to join them infuriated him. His heart raced, and the mix of anger and disbelief running through him made it hard to form words.

"He's totally out." Jason stepped between Gordy and Ethan.

"Oh, no. He will speak for himself." Gordy looked past Jason.

"Okaaay." Jason turned to Ethan and motioned his hands with the "go ahead" motion.

Ethan finally found his voice. "Of course I'm totally out. You're destroying other people to gain power. And I won't be a part of it."

"Suit yourself." Gordy frowned and turned away with a regretful look in his eyes. "Remember, I tried to warn you."

Ethan rolled his eyes. *Yeah, like Gordy really cares*.

With that, Nith lifted his scepter toward the ceiling. The glowing orb was surrounded by purple lightning bolts. Nith released one of the bolts and aimed it straight for Maggie.

Ethan's eyes widened in horror. He dove to stop him, but it was too late. The lightning bolt zapped Maggie's heart, and she looked up. Wisps of the purple light twirled in the air and floated toward the crowd of people against the wall.

"Be careful," Gordy growled through his gritted teeth at Nith.

Nith fired a warning shot from his scepter over Gordy's shoulder. "I know how to manage the power source," he roared. The scepter's light slammed into the wall and shattered into several wisps of light. Again, each wisp gravitated toward the unconscious people.

Gordy's face softened. "I was only reminding you."

Nith ignored Gordy. "Come forward, Maggie."

Maggie immediately rose and stepped slowly over to Nith.

"That's a good girl." Nith patted her head and tapped her forehead with the scepter. Another wisp drifted away. Then he pointed straight at Ethan. "Now. Destroy him."

CHAPTER 25 - Maggie Returns

Jason laughed. "Right, Nith. Like she's going to—oh crap." Jason's eyes widened as Maggie stormed toward them, full force, with her long blonde hair trailing behind her. Jason pulled Ethan back behind him and Brody. "What the heck are you doing, Maggie?"

"Oh, we can't have this," Nith said. He pointed his scepter to the crowd of people. "Nith's army! Awaken." The lightning in the purple orb crackled. Several bolts intertwined together, and the orb glowed brightly. Ethan was sure that if it was nighttime, the orb would light up the entire building. A few wisps of light escaped as the crowd of people stood and closed in on Ethan's friends.

Meanwhile, Maggie continued toward Ethan. She held out her hand, which had one of the laser rings from an earlier level in the game. She glared at Ethan. "I told you I could play too." She aimed the ring at Ethan's head. Ethan braced for the shot of power that would surely hurl toward him, but nothing came.

Instead, Maggie jolted toward him as Gordy tried to grab her arm. Ethan stared in shock as Gordy tripped and crashed into her. She lost her balance but quickly regained her footing and spun around. "Gordy. Seriously?"

"I . . . um . . . be careful with that."

Ethan didn't miss the fact that Gordy stumbled over his words. And he had the same question as Maggie. *What is Gordy doing and what is he hoping to gain? Surely, he didn't interrupt Maggie to tell her to be careful with the ring.*

Maggie rolled her eyes and turned to Ethan, but as she did, the crowd closed in on Alyssa. Jason was doing some impressive fighting moves to fend off his attackers, and Ethan wasn't about to question it. It seemed to be working for him. Drake joined Brody and they fought side by side, disabling their attackers as they closed in on them.

Ethan opened his inventory and grabbed two laser rings, then ran in a zig-zag pattern toward Alyssa. He tossed her one, but she dropped it. Ethan shot a laser at the closest person to Alyssa. The person fell to the ground as Alyssa got her ring and prepared to fight.

Maggie joined the crowd advancing on Alyssa. "Nith said to destroy you, Ethan, but I think taking Alyssa out might do the trick."

Ethan gulped. His heart raced, pumping an insane amount of adrenaline through his veins. He had to remind himself that this wasn't his Maggie. She wouldn't be doing this if she wasn't under Nith's control. This game and Nith's power had changed her. He had to find a way to stop her without hurting her.

Maggie aimed her laser ring at Alyssa, but Alyssa was ready. She fired a shot toward Maggie's feet to throw her off balance. Unfortunately, Maggie saw it coming and dashed to the side. Now it was her turn. She fired her laser, hitting Alyssa in the upper thigh. The force from the laser sent Alyssa flying back, and she slammed into the wall.

"Maggie." Ethan glared at her. "You have to stop." He rushed over to Alyssa. A lump was growing on the back of her head. He lifted Alyssa onto his lap and tried to wake her up. Finally, Alyssa stirred and Ethan let out a sigh of relief. He pulled her up to a sitting position.

"Don't get up before you're ready." Ethan looked at the battle going on in front of them. Lasers shooting. Lights flying. Lightning bolts soaring. "Or until you have to." Alyssa cracked a smile and warmth flowed through him. It felt so much better than those icy, cutting feelings that came with his anger and jealousy.

Maggie rushed forward, bringing Ethan back to the moment at hand. He met her as she stalked toward him and Alyssa. "Maggie, stop. This isn't you. You would never hurt anyone. Ever." Something glistened in Maggie's eye. Was he finally reaching her?

Nith's voice made him jump. "Don't listen to Ethan, Maggie. He wants to win this game. That's all he really cares about."

Maggie's eyes darkened again.

Nith smiled. "Yes. That's right. If you let him go, he will continue to ignore you. He'll be with his friends, his school clubs, and his games."

Ethan glared at Nith. As he stared his rival down, he caught sight of someone emerging from the shadows of the room. Was that Jason and Brody sneaking up? Ethan played it cool, pretending not to see.

Maggie strode past Ethan and headed straight for Alyssa again. He knew he had to do something to stop Maggie. He ran towards her, but he didn't really have a plan. Thoughts were flying through his head, but he couldn't make sense out of any of them. He ran until he collided with Maggie and tackled her to the ground, and both of them landed on their sides.

Nith, still attached to Ganna, gritted his teeth and lifted his scepter to intervene. He aimed it at Alyssa and was about to shoot when Jason lunged at Nith. Nith lost his balance but recovered. Jason took the opportunity and swiped the scepter from Nith. He shot a lightning bolt at Ganna's handcuffs, which immediately released her. Brody lunged for Nith, and they both fell to the ground. Nith curled his knees up to his chest and kicked Brody off of him. Brody immediately leapt to his feet, ready for Nith's attack. This time Nith charged at Brody, but Brody was ready. As Nith reached him, Brody did a sideways kick. Nith jolted back, and Brody went in for a second lunge at Nith. This time, he took Nith to the floor and held him in place. Brody grabbed the cuffs and secured Nith to the stairs.

Jason aimed another lightning bolt at Nith's army and called, "Nith's Army, stand down!" They immediately stopped attacking and sat in place.

Meanwhile, Ethan wrestled Maggie to the ground and flipped her over.

"Let me up," Maggie yelled and struggled to break her wrists free, which Ethan held down firmly.

Ethan shook his head. "I'll let Maggie up. Not Nith's puppet."

Maggie wiggled and squirmed. She pulled an arm free and glared at him. "I'm not his puppet. We are building a better world." She extended her hand, which had the laser ring, but before she could aim it at anyone, Ethan threw his body over her, ripped the ring off her hand, and shoved it in his pocket. He then proceeded to hold Maggie down again.

"Let me up!" she roared.

Ethan shook his head. "Maggie, you don't want to do this. Our world is fine. Our family is fine."

"Says you."

He pushed himself off Maggie but still kept her hands pinned.

Maggie continued. "Do you know how many times we were supposed to do something—hang out, play a game—and you blew me off? Especially since Seeker began?"

Ethan frowned. "I know. I feel terrible. I didn't mean to. This game. It . . . consumes you."

Maggie eyed him.

"No, really. Look at you. You would never dream of hurting anyone. You love my friends, especially Alyssa. If this game didn't consume you too, you'd never do anything like this."

Maggie sighed and turned her head away just as Jason made his way over from his battle with Nith.

"Mags, I'm really sorry," Ethan said.

Brody also came over to them, but he crouched down beside Maggie. "Let her up, Ethan," Brody suggested. Ethan did not think that was a great idea. He knew his sister. Letting her go now was a bad, *bad* idea. He looked at Maggie who had murder in her eyes and then looked at Brody. Brody nodded in reinforcement. "We have the scepter. It's okay."

Okay, Ethan thought. He hoped Brody knew what he was doing.

Ethan let go of Maggie. She immediately sat up, but Brody had her hand. He held it loosely, which seemed to soothe her. He looked in her eyes. "He really is sorry. You were all he talked about this whole time."

Maggie looked doubtful.

"I'm serious," Brody said. "We were trying to focus on getting out alive, and all he could talk about was not letting you down."

Maggie looked at Ethan. Tears started in her eyes. "Really?"

Drake made his way over to them with a cut over his eyebrow

and a bruise on his left arm. "Really," Drake said. "If I had to hear it one more time . . ." Drake held out his pointer finger.

Everyone nodded, and then Maggie started to cry. First, it was one tear. Followed by another. And another, until she let out a sob. She sat up and wrapped her arms around Ethan, sobbing harder. Ethan breathed a sigh of relief. For the first time since this nightmare started, he had his sister back, and he was not going to let anything happen to her again.

Jason put down the scepter and joined the hug. "Aww, I just love happy endings!" He reached his arm out and pulled Brody in too.

Maggie coughed and they all separated. Ethan snuck a sideways glance and saw Maggie's cheeks flush pink. He shook his head then turned to Drake and pointed at his cut. "What happened to you?"

"Oh, nothing," Jason answered for Drake with a wave of his hand. "After Brody lasered Ganna free with this—" he branded the scepter "—we tackled the Purple Pscyho."

"Enough of this," Nith roared from behind the group.

"How'd you—" Jason asked.

Nith strode toward Ethan, Maggie, Jason, and Brody, dangling the handcuffs in front of him. "You think this would stop me?" He threw his head back and laughed tauntingly. "I created this!"

Gordy stood several feet away, but Ethan noticed his arms were stiff and his fists were clenched. He also noticed Gordy made no effort to join Nith.

"That was a fun tussle with Jason and Brody, but now it's time to get serious."

Ethan and Maggie rushed to their feet with Alyssa. They all stood together, ready for whatever Nith threw their way.

"I'm done waiting around." Nith eyed the group. "The Merge will happen tonight."

"No offense," Jason said, "but you're no more powerful now than you were earlier. So I don't see how 'The Merge' will happen at all."

Nith laughed again. He held out his scepter, and its orb was now the size of an oversized beach ball. He walked over to the center of the room where the wooden platform stood. He placed the orb on top and it stood unwaveringly on display.

"My orb of power continues to grow, does it not?"

Jason gulped.

"Each person who plays this game and gets trapped in here adds to my growing power. In fact"—he glared at Gordy—"Gordy should be tricking more players while I deal with all of you."

Gordy scowled, then snapped his fingers and vanished.

Nith nodded in approval. "This game has tripled in popularity since you became stuck here. With each passing minute, more and more players are 'souled' to me when they continue to return to me. Then, more and more get stuck here, which in turn . . ." He looked right at Ethan.

"Grows the power in the orb," Ethan finished for him.

"Exactly." Nith clicked his tongue. "Such a pity. So smart, but you don't realize what you are throwing away." He twirled his empty scepter in his hand. "This orb will continue to grow until it fills this entire building. Once that happens, the orb will explode, causing a rip in the veil between the digital world and your world. It is then that people will recognize my power. I will rule over the new world where I will finally get the recognition I deserve." He dipped his scepter into the now truck-sized orb. The orb shrunk a fraction, but then the scepter had a new purple orb on top.

"Let's keep track of how many are locked in this game right now." He held out the scepter and shot a lightning bolt in the air. Purple wisps strayed toward the crowd of Nith's prisoners. A digital counter appeared in the air. It started at one million and rapidly counted up. The numbers were changing so fast, Ethan couldn't keep track of it.

Ethan pulled Drake aside. "Go back to the Grand Hall."

"What? Why?"

Ethan held out his hand. "It's important. I need you to warn every single player who logs in about what is going on. Tell them to leave the game immediately. If they insist on staying, recruit them."

"Recruit them," Drake repeated.

Ethan nodded. "This is an attack on our world. We need an army to help us."

Alyssa placed a hand on Ethan's back. "Yes. An army. Ethan's Army."

"Be careful." Drake pointed to them. Then, he turned and dashed out the door.

CHAPTER 26 - Nith's Reveal

The numbers on Nith's soul counter continued to rise at lightning speed.

Right as Drake left, Nith spotted him, but it was too late. By the time he aimed the scepter, Drake was gone.

"Yes." Brody pumped his fist. "Something went right for a change."

That lasted about a second because Nith then focused on Ethan. He aimed the scepter and released a purple bolt of power. Brody leaped at Ethan, shoving both of them out of the path of Nith's shot.

"Look." Jason pointed at the purple wisps of light traveling toward the crowd of people. "They're moving again. I thought we knocked 'em all out."

Ganna emerged from the shadows and joined them. She spoke for the first time. "The light has been doing this the whole time. It always gravitates toward the trapped people."

"Oh, good catch, Jason," Alyssa said and flashed a smile his way. "Keep an eye on them so they can't sneak up on us."

Jason nodded. "On it." He waved his hand.

Ethan frowned. He wished he had Jason's charm. He tried to shove the uncomfortable feeling in his stomach deep down inside. He had to focus on the right things or they'd never get out of there. Alyssa and Jason were right. The people were stirring and waking.

Nith scowled at Ganna. "I told you before," she said to Nith, "every time you use your power, you release the souls you have stored in the orb."

Ethan looked at the big orb on the platform, which was only slightly smaller.

"Shut up," Nith snapped back.

"'Shut up?'" Jason echoed in a questioning tone from his post by the prisoners. "Dude, she hasn't even said a word up until now."

More people were starting to wake up.

Jason looked confident to Ethan, but something seemed different this time from where he stood. Before, the people seemed like they were in a trance. Now, their eyes were clear and their movements smooth. Alyssa noticed too and ran over to them, asking if they were okay. As she crouched down to talk to someone sitting on the ground, Ethan caught Nith aiming his scepter at Alyssa. "Alyssa. Watch out!"

Alyssa spun around and blocked her body by crossing her arms outward in front of her. Purple light headed straight for her. She lifted her hand instinctively. The light caught her ring. For a minute, the light lingered, frozen. Then, it broke free from the ring and bounced back toward Nith. The force knocked him to the ground. The light then bounced off the floor and exploded, sending fragments all over the room. They reached the people, causing them to stir more. Nith was still lying on the ground. Brody and Maggie ran over to Nith, and Brody picked up the scepter. He aimed it at the ceiling, and the lightning bolt broke into eight streams of light, which landed in an oval formation around Nith like a cage.

Ethan turned to Ganna. "Get out of here, now. Drake went to the Grand Hall. Stay there."

"No." Ganna stood firm. "I will help you fight."

"If you really want to help," Brody said, walking closer to her, "please go. Nith will have no problem using you against Drake again. Especially trapped like this."

Ganna's face softened. "Okay. I'll do this for Drake." She handed Ethan the Guardian chain she once wore. "But take this. If you need help, hold this up to the orb of light. Hold it tightly between both hands. It will glow and light up. That will send me a distress signal." Then, she turned and left.

Ethan ran over to Alyssa who was sitting on the ground from the impact. He knelt by her side. "Are you okay?"

She nodded and brushed her hair out of her eyes. Her ring glimmered a bright purple, the same shade as the orbs of light. Ethan pointed to her hand.

She held it up in front of her face, examining both sides of her hand and catching every angle she could of the ring. "It's *purple*."

Jason ran over. "Yo, dude. You got her a ring? *Now*?" His grin widened, probably in response to Alyssa's mortified reaction.

Maggie was halfway across the room, but she must have heard because she covered her mouth and giggled.

Ethan opened his mouth to interrupt, but Jason held out his palm. "Okay, Mr. Smooth. Where's mine?"

Man, it was hard to talk to Jason when he was on a roll. "Look. It's not what you thi—" Ethan tried.

"Hey, Brody," Jason called. "You have to come over here. Ethan's getting us rings."

Brody took a few steps before resting the scepter against a wall and joining the rest of Team Dynamite.

"No, I'm not." Ethan felt his face flush.

"Aww, c'mon. We'll get it inscribed with E.A.—Ethan's Army."

Ethan so wished he had something to throw at Jason.

Alyssa pointed to the orb. "This ring blocked Nith's attack. It must have absorbed some of the power."

"Oooohhhh," everyone said together.

"C'mon, we have to figure out what to do with Nith," Brody said, turning his head toward the stairs.

Ethan was about to move when he noticed the cage of light had disappeared. Instead of being trapped inside, Nith stood free by the crowd of people, scepter in hand.

"You fools used this carelessly." Nith waved the scepter in the air. "Just look how much power I lost."

Ethan was slightly reassured. *Maybe we can trick him into freeing more souls by using the scepter,* he thought. It seemed like a good idea until he looked at the digital counter. There were millions of people still trapped and under Nith's control. There was no way he could trick Nith into releasing his power that much. They had to come up with a different way.

"Ethan." Drake's voice boomed from the entrance. Everyone turned and looked at Drake who had Gordy by the arm. It looked like Drake had held him like that for a while. "I found him trying to lure more people into the game. I was able to disarm him and bring him back."

Drake was about to say more, but Nith raised his scepter and stormed toward Drake.

"Failed again, eh, Gordy?" Nith aimed the scepter at Drake's hand, causing him to lose his grip. Nith shot another bolt of light. This time it lifted Gordy in the air and pulled him to Nith. Nith released the power and Gordy dropped to the ground in front of him. "I gave you one job," Nith roared. "You have become even more useless than you were before."

He pulled Gordy to his feet and tossed him to the side in front of the trapped gamers against the wall. "I have no reason to keep you around." Nith raised his scepter and aimed at Gordy.

"Ah-ah-ahhh." Gordy wagged a finger at Nith. "You wouldn't want to get rid of your *apprentice* in this game would you?" His voice dripped with venom. "I suggest you lower your scepter before things get . . . ugly." His piercing glare caused Nith to lower his weapon slightly. Only slightly, until he recovered.

"You are in *no* position to threaten me."

Jason positioned himself between Ethan and Alyssa, draping his arms around their shoulders. "Anyone else enjoying the fact that our two villains are ready to take each other out? My bet's on Gordy. He's small but feisty."

"Really, Nith?" Gordy moved away from the crowd of people and backed up toward the stairs. He stepped slowly, daring Nith to stop him. Instead, Nith offered a half-smile. Gordy reached for one of the security mirrors hanging on the wall without taking his eyes off Nith. "I'm tired of you treating me like a useless pawn." He lifted the mirror off the wall. "It's time everyone knows who you really are!"

Nith snorted. Whatever Gordy was about to disclose didn't seem to bother Nith at all. In fact, he shot another light from his scepter, which knocked the mirror out of Gordy's hand. He shot a second time. This time the force knocked Gordy off his feet. "You must be dumber than that one." He pointed at Jason.

"Hey," Jason protested with a stomp on the ground. He recovered quickly. "Speak for yourself. I'm not the one ready to take on a very ticked off gnome."

Gordy leapt to his feet and snapped his fingers. The rest of the security mirrors on the walls floated off their hooks and lingered in the air. They surrounded the room so that no matter what direction you faced, you could see the face of the mirrors.

"Whatever you think you have to reveal about me will show even worse on you." Nith fired a third shot at Gordy as Gordy leapt behind one of the floating mirrors. The purple beam of light bounced off the mirror and headed right back toward Nith, striking his arm that held the scepter. Wisps of light floated away toward the crowd of people. Nith fumbled with the scepter for a second but gained control. The face of the mirror rippled, erasing the reflection of the room and instead revealing a small office with gaming equipment resting on the desk.

Ethan and his friends exchanged looks, except for Drake.

"That room," Drake said in a low whisper. "I know that room." Drake frowned, turning his face away. Maggie reached over and patted his arm.

Nith clicked his tongue. "Clearly, you have decided to side with that traitor." Nith pointed at Drake. He shook his head. "Though I shouldn't be surprised. It's not like this is the first time you betrayed me."

Gordy glared at Nith. "Now, now. Is that any way to talk about . . . your nephew?"

Ethan looked at Drake. All color drained from Drake's face.

Gordy locked eyes with Nith and said, "Security Mirror, who is Lord Nith?"

The mirror continued to show the room with the small office, but this time someone walked in. He wasn't facing the mirror. All Ethan could see was the back of a tall figure with long brown hair. He sat down at his desk and grabbed a gaming box and a controller. He moved his mouse to wake up the computer. The following message displayed: "Good morning. Type in your password to continue."

The man typed: "I am Lord Nith."

Another message appeared: "Thank you, Ronald. You may proceed."

He typed in some long code strings on his computer and attached a USB cable between the computer and the gaming box. Electrical currents zipped and zapped and crackled. The force lifted the console slightly. Purple light beams poured from every crack in the console. A bright purple glow filled the room, then slowly reduced down to nothing. The currents stopped, and the console returned calmly back on the desk. But when everything settled, the room was empty. Ronald was gone.

CHAPTER 27 - Gordy

"*You're* Ronald?" Ethan blurted when the security mirror went dark and the face returned to a normal reflection. "As in Ronald Tinim? As in Drake's *Uncle Ron*?" Ethan turned to Drake.

Drake nodded, still looking pale. Ethan, Maggie, Jason, Alyssa, and Brody gathered around him. Drake stepped away from them. His stare poured through Nith as he strode across the room. He finally spoke, coming inches within Nith. "That's what it looks like. Why? Why would you do this?"

Nith raised his scepter. "I don't want to hurt you. Why do you think I allowed you to be the Guardian?" He aimed it straight at Drake. "But I will if I have to."

"You didn't answer my question, *Ron*." Drake's voice dripped with venom.

Nith ignored him, still aiming his scepter. Drake took several steps back.

Ethan peeked at the digital counter of trapped souls. He frowned at the way the numbers were still growing. His heart raced. He had to do something. But what? What could he do to stop someone so evil he'd destroy his own nephew?

As if reading his mind, Gordy shouted, "Your sword." Ethan looked at him for a minute, wondering why Gordy would help him, but he would worry about that later. He opened his inventory and reached for the sword.

Nith held the scepter steady. "It's a shame it has come to this. You were supposed to be part of this beautiful transformation."

"Get back," Brody called to Drake as Nith stepped forward.

"Catch," Ethan called and tossed the sword to Drake. Drake caught it easily and flipped it around.

Nith released a shot of light from the scepter, but Drake was too quick. The sword blocked the purple light just as it reached him. The beam deflected off the sword

Drake held the sword upright in his hands and closed in on Nith, who stood by the giant purple orb of power in the room. It was now the size of a truck. Brody and Jason ran up behind Nith. Everyone else, including Gordy, joined them in a circle surrounding Nith.

Drake pointed the sword at Nith, but Nith wasn't going down without a fight. He fired another shot from the scepter, however Drake was too quick and blocked it. He swiped at Nith, knocking the scepter out of his hands. Brody and Jason immediately rushed on Nith and pinned his arms behind his back. Gordy ran and grabbed the scepter.

Ethan stood frozen. What was Gordy was about to do? Whose side was he on? Then, Gordy aimed the scepter straight at Nith. Nith laughed and wriggled his right arm free. He stretched it out and his fingers grazed the orb. "You are an even bigger traitor than Drake is. But you aren't as innocent as you pretend to be."

With that, Gordy fired a shot at Nith. Purple light hit him in the chest. Instantly, purple lightning crept across his body to where his right hand brushed the orb. He immediately slumped to the ground. Brody and Jason let go of Nith and rushed over to Ethan.

Gordy's face fell. There was an invisible battle going on inside Gordy. Ethan felt the struggle. Slowly, Gordy handed the scepter to Ethan. A long pause hung in the air before Gordy spoke. He looked at Ethan and Maggie. "He called me a traitor. Maybe so. But, it's what a father does for his children," he said quietly. He pulled his gaze away from Ethan and his sister.

"Wait. What?" Jason's eyes widened.

Ethan's thoughts echoed Jason's response. *What in the world do Gordy's kids have to do with any of this? Why did he look at us when he said this?*

"I don't know why you're looking at us," Maggie said, hands on her hips. "We wouldn't know. Our father disappeared years ago. And I'm pretty sure he isn't a gnome."

"When I was brought into the game by him," Gordy said and pointed to Nith, "he made my avatar a gnome. It was his world after all." He shifted his weight. "But the person behind the avatar is Aiden. Aiden Bradford." He lowered his eyes, avoiding Ethan's stare. "I really am your father." Finally, he pulled his gaze and looked Ethan in the eyes.

Ethan could barely process what was going on. *Gordy? Er, Aiden? Father? Impossible.* But then he thought about all those times when Gordy could have destroyed him but didn't. His hint about the sword made more sense to him now. Was this really why?

Gordy continued, "Back in the Shadow Room, I knew Nith wanted to destroy you. He had to. He was about to be discovered. So, when I stole the scepter, I willed the magic to take you all to the maze. As you can tell"—Gordy pointed to Nith—"my defiance displeases him greatly."

Alyssa gasped and covered her mouth. She rushed over and hugged Ethan and Maggie. "It's okay," she said. "It'll be okay."

Ethan felt numb. *How can it be okay? Drake's Uncle Ron is Lord Nith and I'm supposed to believe my dad is his sidekick Gordy?* He felt that familiar heat rise up from his chest. His body shook with rage. "You didn't think to tell us this when we first got here?"

Gordy moved closer to him. "I couldn't. I was under complete control of Nith."

"And what about when he held me captive?" Maggie glared at Gordy. "You let your daughter be a prisoner to this . . . " She waved her hand in the air. "This thing?"

"And all those times we had to battle you," Brody added. "I don't care what threat I would be up against, I'd never allow Nith to do this to my friends—let alone my kids."

"And stealing my grandmother's ring," Alyssa added.

"And the *maze*." Ethan's voice was a roar now. He grabbed the scepter from Gordy. "You created a tree monster with this that tried to kill me! Way to go, *Dad*." More rage pulsed through his veins. He couldn't think of anything besides the frustration in his heart. He looked at the scepter in his hand. Every problem. Every missing person. Every danger was due to this. He tossed the scepter to the side. He couldn't even look at it.

Gordy hung his head. "I didn't have the ability to defy him yet. Like I said, I sent you to the maze. It was your best chance of survival. But my loyalty had to seem real to Nith. He had to believe I could be trusted. The tables have turned now and, like Ganna, I'm finally free."

"Uh, guys," Jason interrupted.

Nobody responded. All eyes were focused on Ethan and Gordy.

Drake rushed forward, pointing his finger at Gordy. "Don't

you *dare* compare yourself to Ganna! She was his prisoner." He held up his wrists in front of his own face. "She was handcuffed to him."

"G-guys." Jason raised his voice, but still, nothing.

Gordy tilted his head. "She wasn't when you were in the Throne Room." He pointed to Drake's neck. "You know, when she took that from you."

Drake scowled.

"My guess is that Nith controlled her by threatening you. He knows how to manipulate. And if that doesn't work, he uses his power."

"Really. Guys. Look—" Desperation filled Jason's voice, but it was no use.

Ethan was aware of Jason's pleas, but he couldn't make himself listen. He had to understand why Gordy—er, his dad or whoever he was—would do this. As the conversation went on, a shiver ran down Ethan's spine. What Gordy said made sense. Wasn't that what happened with Maggie when she was ordered to destroy him? She was completely under Nith's control. It was as if it wasn't her there at all.

"Have you been here the whole time?" Ethan asked.

Gordy nodded.

"What happened? How did you end up here?"

"Guys." Jason's voice echoed through the room. "Guys. Guys. Guys. Stop and listen to me!"

Ethan's anger returned. "This is important. I need to know this. Now, back off."

Jason's eyes watered, but he took a deep breath. "Fine," he said flatly. "Suit yourself."

He stalked across the room and leaned against the wall by the entrance.

Gordy continued his explanation. "I have done things before that I am not proud of." He looked at Maggie and then Ethan. "Though I don't regret them. Because if I never married your mother, you two wouldn't be here." He took a deep breath. "But, I betrayed my best friend, Ronald."

"Yeah," Drake interrupted. "They got the story on how you stole his notes and then his girlfriend." He shook his head.

"Yes, well," Gordy continued, "he caught up with me one day. Said he wanted to put the past behind us and be friends again. I thought I could finally make amends for the hurt and pain I caused. We went to dinner one night and it was like old times. Talking about our favorite games, buddies from school, and what we have been up to since we last saw each other. When dinner was through, he said he wanted to show me this new game he was working on. He wanted my input. He said it was going to be the next big thing. So, I went with him. When we got there, he opened the game, Seeker, that he had finished developing. He showed me the layout of the fortress and the rules on advancing in the game. Then he said that the game was the first of its kind. He gave me the Transport headset. He plugged one end of the USB cord to the computer and one to the console. He typed in a password. I was instantly transported into the game—the same way every player is."

"I'm going to try one more time," Jason called from his spot at the wall.

"Shhh," Ethan, Brody, Drake, Alyssa, and Maggie called in unison.

Jason threw his hands in the air. "I give up." Ethan heard him run off somewhere. Before he could look, Gordy continued his story. "I was never able to leave after that. Nith showed up shortly after. And then you, Drake. I was given a choice: serve him as his apprentice or be imprisoned in the game forever. That's when I realized Ronald never forgave me like he said he did. He was planning his revenge. And no matter what I chose, I knew I'd still be trapped here forever."

Ethan breathed deeply. After all these years of wondering what he did to make his dad leave, after years of grief and pain, after years of helping his mom move on and live a normal life—his father never abandoned them. He was fighting this whole time to get back to them. A tear formed in the corner of Ethan's eyes. A knot formed in his throat.

Don't cry. Don't cry, he told himself. As he tried to pull himself together, a soft touch on his shoulder soothed his nerves. He expected it to be Maggie, but when he turned to see who it was, it was Alyssa. She stood there and said nothing, but she kept her hand on his shoulder. Then, she pulled him into a hug. For that one minute, everything was fine. There was no Seeker. They weren't trapped anywhere. His life wasn't just turned upside down. There was no anger or jealousy. He wanted to hide there forever. He was so tired. But he needed to end this. He needed to get everyone out of there and truly move on. So, he gently pulled back out of the hug. "Thank you," he whispered.

He looked at Maggie who sat crouched on the floor. Brody scooted down to her level and had a consoling arm around her shoulders. A loud crash sounded, interrupting the moment. Ethan turned just in time to see Jason, who stood face to face with Nith. Both had their hands on the scepter. Nith shoved Jason back and ripped the scepter out of his hands.

"Take cover." Jason's voice was a shriek and he ran toward Ethan. "I tried to warn you."

A powerful stream of purple light ripped through the air.

"As sweet as this is," Nith said triumphantly, "we have some business to take care of." The light reached the tower's ceiling and split into hundreds of factions of light, showering the people Nith had trapped against the walls.

Jason scowled and waved a pointing finger at everyone. "While you all were ignoring me, Nith got the scepter that *someone*"—he rolled his eyes for effect— "threw to the side, and he regained control of his army." He then pointed to Nith as he levitated off the ground with purple energy surrounding him.

Ethan looked up in horror.

"Seekers," Nith called from high above them, "attack."

CHAPTER 28 - The Growing Orb

Nith fired another burst of light at the crowd of people. They obediently rose and advanced on Ethan and his friends.

"What are we going to do now?" Brody asked. "We're outnumbered."

Jason nodded.

"We keep fighting," Drake said.

Everyone reached in their inventories to find something to fight off their attackers. Jason stuck to his own devices and did several sidekicks, jumps, and twirls. Ethan grinned. Jason looked like an anime superhero. He felt a twinge of guilt at the feelings of jealousy and anger he had toward him.

Alyssa and Brody used their laser rings to keep their attackers at bay.

Ethan reached in his pocket and pulled out the Guardian Key. Ganna's earlier words echoed in his head: *"If you need help, hold this up to the orb of light. Hold it tightly between both hands. It will glow and light up. That will send me a distress signal."*

He thought twice about calling her, but as he watched the army of people swarming around his friends, he knew he needed all the help he could get. This had to work. They were running out of options.

He ran across the room and held the key toward the large orb.

"Oh, no you don't," Nith shouted and fired a shot. Ethan gulped as the beam aimed straight at him. It shot through the air right at the middle of his forehead. He held up the Guardian Key to his forehead, trying to take up as much space as possible. The purple light hurling toward him struck the key, blocking Nith's attack.

The impact sent Ethan flying backwards, and he skidded across the floor. He sat up and examined the key, which began to glow. "Perfect," he whispered.

He scrambled back up on his feet and glanced around for something—anything—to block more shots. An armored shield decorating the wall hung half off. Ethan snatched it up and shielded himself from more and more shots coming his way. He couldn't tell how his friends were doing against the Seekers, but he crossed his fingers that they had it under control. He raced toward a metal knight in the corner. He leapt behind it and found Gordy there.

Even though he didn't quite reach the orb in the room, the sword had caught the power from blocking Nith's shot. It had to be enough.

Ethan crouched down, making sure to block as much of himself as possible.

"I'll cover you," Gordy said. With a knowing smile, he snapped his fingers. Several dinner plates appeared, just like the ones in the dining room. One by one, the plates lifted in the air and positioned themselves in the line of fire. Ethan couldn't help himself. As much as he didn't want to, he had to smile at that.

Ethan held the Guardian Key with both hands.

"C'mon, c'mon, c'mon," he urged.

A little spark of warmth grew, then fizzled out. It was as if the key tried to do what Ethan needed but didn't have enough oomph. The shots from Nith weren't enough. Ethan knew what he had to do.

"Keep him busy," he whispered to Gordy.

Gordy had no time to argue. Within seconds, Ethan sped to the center of the room. He crouched down behind the large orb. It was still growing despite the amount of power Nith was using. Maybe Ganna was wrong about that. Or maybe more people were still being trapped despite Drake's efforts. He shivered at the thought.

Still crouching low, Ethan lifted the key to the orb. Since it was so massive, he didn't have far to reach. As soon as the key touched the light, the entire room dimmed, then returned to normal. Ethan sat back against the stand. He held the key in his hands. A tingling sensation began. The key grew warmer and warmer, until it was so warm, he let go. The key lifted up from his hands and glowed. The light that poured from the key shot out in every direction with blinding brightness. Seconds later, the light faded, the key returned to his hand, and the warmth left it. He got up to leave and ran right into Nith.

So much for Gordy covering him. Ethan craned his neck, scanning the room. Gordy was nowhere. He should have known not to trust him. Dad or not.

Nith gabbed Ethan's arm and pulled him in front of the orb. "Finally," Nith said, "these games can stop."

As Nith raised his scepter to Ethan, Ganna ran through the entrance, followed by a crowd of people. Players. Seekers. "Ethan's Army. Let's do this."

"Let's do this," the crowd's thunderous voice rang out.

Ethan's Army poured through the room, battling one on one with Nith's Seekers. Lasers were fired. Fists were thrown. People were shoved.

Nith's hold on Ethan did not loosen. Thoughts raced through Ethan's mind. *If I can only catch him off guard.* As if on cue, a dining room plate lunged toward Nith. Ethan smiled. That had to be Gordy. He took full advantage and yanked himself free from Nith's hold. He scrambled away as Nith charged toward Gordy.

"I've had about enough of you." In one fluid move, Nith fired his scepter at Gordy. The light hit him in the chest. His eyes widened and his arm reached out as if trying to stop the light charging at him. Light radiated from where Gordy was struck and traveled through him. The light lifted Gordy in the air and turned him to stone.

"What?" Ethan shrieked and fell to the floor. "Noooo."

Nith then turned his weapon on Alyssa, who had been helping Ethan's Army take over Nith's Seekers. Ethan glared at Nith. Nith had taken his friend, his sister, and now, for the second time, his dad. There was no way he would let Nith get away with it. Not again. With all the strength and courage he could muster up, Ethan charged at Nith and tackled him. Both tumbled to the ground. Nith grabbed Ethan's arm, but Ethan wriggled it free and threw himself on top of Nith.

"Guys! Help me restrain him."

Jason, Brody, and Drake were already on their way over while Ethan kept Nith pinned with his elbow and snatched the scepter with his other hand.

Drake arrived first and lifted Nith to his feet. Brody and Jason followed and helped keep Nith restrained, his arms pinned behind his back. Nith was having none of it and kicked backwards right into Brody's shin. Brody loosened his grip and Nith broke free from him. He shoved Jason to the side, knocking him into the stand holding the orb.

Nith leapt toward Ethan, who jumped to the side. Nith missed him and tumbled to the floor instead.

Ethan aimed the scepter at Nith. He wasn't sure how it worked, but he had noticed that Nith always had it do what he wanted it to do. Maybe it worked like his sword did. Nith crawled backwards trying to escape the range of fire. Ethan fired a warning shot in the air. *It worked,* he thought. Nith froze.

"I don't want to hurt you." Ethan's aim was still on Nith. "So don't make me. Get up." Nith jumped to his feet. Drake and Jason descended on him, grabbing his arms.

"Quick," Ganna said. "Destroy it." She pointed to the scepter in Ethan's hand.

"How do I—"

"Just do it. He's powerless without it. Without the magic. Let the souls go free."

Ethan nodded. He summoned all the feelings of frustration and anger he had harbored all his life over a father he thought had abandoned him. He lifted the scepter over his head, ready to smash it into the ground, but it didn't feel like enough. It wasn't powerful enough.

What could empower him more than those feelings?

Maggie walked over to him and held his hand. Alyssa joined her. Then Brody. He was reminded of the warm fuzzy feelings he got when he thought of Alyssa and how her hug earlier empowered him to go on. He thought about Maggie's ability to forgive him and how it was stronger than any magical control Nith had over her. He thought about Brody, his best friend through thick and thin. He thought about Jason and his ability to look for the fun and humorous side of things instead of letting anger and rage take over. He thought about Drake and Gordy and how choosing the right thing to do freed them both. He thought about all those relationships. His heart swelled and warmth flowed through him. With all his might, he threw the scepter to the ground. Ethan expected it to shatter, but it didn't.

"Look what you've done," Nith screamed. He broke free and huddled by the large orb in the room. "It's leaking power."

A tiny hairline fracture crawled around the scepter's orb of power, but that was it. The purple power escaped as much as it could through the thin crack, which wasn't much. Alyssa's ring glowed purple in response to the tiny fibers escaping from the scepter.

"Your ring," Ethan said. "Didn't it catch one of Nith's shots?"

Alyssa nodded.

"Does it shoot? Like a laser ring?"

Alyssa licked her lips. "I don't know. I'll try." She took a deep breath and aimed her ring at the scepter. A purple beam of light left the ring and crashed into the scepter. The hairline fracture in the orb grew wider. It slowly grew bigger with each passing second. Round and round it went. Bigger and bigger it grew until the glass broke away and all the light left the orb.

As the power escaped, it once again reached the original Seekers trapped by Nith, awakening them.

"Seekers, quick." Jason waved them on. "Go to the chamber. You're free. Go home."

The crowd obeyed. Ethan wasn't sure, but he thought he saw someone who looked like Max in the crowd heading home.

"It doesn't matter," Nith said. He waved a hand over the orb, which was now so large that Ethan could feel its energy from where he stood. "I have all the power here that I need. They may be leaving, but even more have been brought in. As you can see, my supply is as plentiful as ever."

He held his hands over the orb, summoning its power. Purple lightning swirled around the orb, responding to Nith's call. It glowed and lifted off the platform. As it hovered, Ethan shivered, a sense of dread overcoming him.

CHAPTER 29 - The Black Hole

"Stop him," Drake yelled. He advanced on Nith and grabbed his cloak, but it was too late.

"Great Orb of Power: Transform!" Nith lifted his hands upwards and the orb followed.

The magical force was so strong it created a tunnel of wind. Ethan felt it brush over him, blowing his wavy hair to the side. Higher and higher the orb went until it reached the ceiling. The orb hovered there, rotating in place. As it spun, its color changed. It turned from the usual bright purple to a deeper purple, growing darker and darker until it was pure black and no longer a sphere.

"Great," Jason's voice cracked. "We have a spinning black hole in the middle of The Keep." He pushed his hair out of his eyes. "What could possibly go wrong?"

Drake's face drained of color. Panic replaced it. "We gotta get out of here. Now!"

As Drake said this, the cloud stopped spinning and the wind stopped blowing. Everything was still. Too still, like the calm before a nasty storm.

"Don't let him leave." Brody pointed at Nith who now stood at the entrance.

Alyssa jumped in front of Nith and aimed her ring at

Nith's foot. A beam of light hurled toward him. He fell to the ground—again. Brody and Jason picked him off the floor—again.

Jason grinned. "No offense, but you stumble a lot for a villain."

That comment earned Jason a glare, but there was nothing else Nith could do about it. Nith ripped an arm away from Brody, but Jason tackled him to the ground.

Then, the atmosphere in the room changed. There was a strong pull as if someone turned on a monster of a vacuum. Ethan looked in the direction of the pull. The security mirrors effortlessly flew toward the black cloud.

Nith laughed. "It started. There's nothing you can do." He looked at Ethan. "You should have joined me when you had the chance."

More and more things were pulled toward the cloud—the armors, the knights, the decorations, the drapes, the keys on the drapes. The more that was pulled in, the stronger the pull became.

"Grab on to the stairs," Ethan called, yelling over the roar of the black cloud. He wasn't sure who heard him at first because it seemed even his words were pulled into the cloud, but his friends and Maggie must have, because within a minute everyone was at the steps, huddled together.

Everyone except Jason and Nith.

"How are we going to stop this," Alyssa asked. "We can't hold on like this forever. And we can't leave Jason like that."

Drake frowned. "This might not work, but it could be our only shot. This hole was created by the power—er, souls Nith stole from his Seekers."

Instantly Ethan understood and nodded in agreement. The

only thing that could counteract that power was an equally opposing force. "You're on to something. Alyssa, does your ring still glow purple?"

She nodded.

"Okay, my guess is that as long as it glows purple, there's still some power to it."

An armored shield whizzed by his head toward the cloud. He ducked, narrowly avoiding impact. "Since the cloud was created by the same power, maybe it can destroy the cloud."

Ethan looked at Jason and Nith on the floor. Jason still had Nith pinned. His arms and chest were on top of Nith, but the pull lifted Jason's legs in the air.

Alyssa gulped at the scene in front of her. "I'm on it." She let go of her hold on the railing, using both hands to aim. Struggling against the pull, she held out her ring and fired at the cloud. She blushed. "I feel ridiculous shooting at this thing," she shouted.

Ethan caught her eye. "You could never be ridiculous." He immediately regretted it. He could have kicked himself. *Definitely not the time. Maybe she didn't hear me because the force of the wind is so deafening.* But when he looked over, he saw her blush turn a deeper shade of red. She shook her head and fired again at the cloud.

The pull of the cloud grew stronger. Alyssa fought against the pull, but it kept moving her closer, little by little, away from the stairs—and her friends.

As hard as Alyssa tried to fight it, Ethan could see the pull was stronger. He'd already seen things happen to Max and Maggie. He wasn't going to sit there and let it happen to Alyssa too. He held out his hand. "Hand me the ring. You need to grab on to something." Alyssa nodded. She inched her way over to him, and with each step, she leaned into the overbearing wind. The wind's force fought back, but Alyssa continued to persevere. She finally made it over and gave Ethan the ring.

He fired at the cloud, willing it to close. It shrunk a little bit, but the pull still grew stronger. Various objects kept disappearing into the blackness. That's when Gordy's life-size statue lifted.

Ethan turned his attention back to the cloud. He kept firing, one after another. He stopped when Gordy's statue was hoisted in the air. Powered by the pull of the cloud, the statue hurled toward the powerful void.

Ethan didn't know what to do. He wanted to save Gordy's statue. If he did, there was a possibility of getting Gordy—his dad—back, along with the answers he needed. But they were still faced with the cloud that was sure to devour them all.

Ethan fired at the cloud again, hoping that he could close it before Gordy disappeared. It became clear that wasn't going to happen. The cloud continued to close, but at a slow pace. Meanwhile, the statue lurched toward the hole at an alarming speed.

He had to get the statue away.

He considered using the power from the ring, hoping he could use it to pull Gordy back. It was a huge risk, though, because it could destroy the statue in the process, sealing Gordy's fate. But he had to try. It was that very light that had turned him to stone. Maybe it would counteract the effect, like it was doing to the hole. After all, if the ring worked on a force that strong, surely it could undo Nith's damage.

He fired the ring at the statue. The light reached it, then vanished. Small cracks emanated from the point of impact, but the statue was still intact. He had to find a way to use the light to pull the statue toward them.

He aimed the ring again.

"Focus." Drake's voice boomed over the noisy wind. "Tell the power what to do."

Ethan nodded. He aimed again, focusing on nothing but the ring's power and Gordy's statue. He imagined a strong rope attached to the statue and fired. This time, the light struck the statue and wrapped around it like a glowing purple lasso. More tiny cracks covered Gordy. Ethan really hoped he was doing the right thing and not destroying Gordy.

Ethan pulled his arm backwards as if pulling a real rope toward him. The statue slowly moved back. Little by little, the statue inched toward the stairs. It wasn't easy, as the strength of the cloud intensified. Then, he turned back to the hole. He fired Alyssa's ring at the vast cloud of energy. He hoped it was enough, as pulling Gordy back to them took an immense amount of power.

He continued firing, still holding the railing with one hand and shooting with the other. Just as any other time the power was used, wisps of the energy returned to trapped players in the game. More and more players could be freed. He hoped everyone made it out. If he could disable the cloud, then every player trapped should be released—in theory.

"Brody," Ethan called over his shoulder. "Hold onto Gordy."

"You got it." He pulled the statue closer to him and held on tightly.

The cloud continued to shrink slowly.

Ethan's eyes turned to Jason. Why was he still on the ground with Nith? "Get out of there," Ethan yelled. "It's going to pull you in."

"I can't," Jason yelled back.

"He'll get away. We can't let him get away."

"Get out of there," Ethan repeated.

"No," Jason screamed. "I'll hold him down. You try to get that thing closed." As frustrated as Ethan was with Jason before with his close friendship with Alyssa, this had to take the cake. Why was he being so stubborn? Did he not think Ethan would go get him? Ethan may have been jealous of Jason earlier, but he was also a good friend. A loyal friend. A person. Ethan would get him out of there, even if it was the last thing he did.

"You fool," Nith croaked at Jason. "You'll get us both killed."

Ethan's mind raced. There had to be a way to help Jason. There had to be a way to stop him from being sucked into the cloud. It was gaining on them.

Ethan clung to the railing of the stairs as a particularly strong pull rattled him. If only Jason had something to hold on to. Maybe if Ethan stretched his arm out, he could grab Jason's hand. And then it hit him. There was just about everyone from Team Dynamite on these railings.

"We're going to form a human chain," Ethan said to his friends. "We'll start with Brody. Maggie, grab his hand. The rest of you, continue to extend the chain by holding on to the person's hand before you. Whatever you do, don't let go or we could be that cloud's dinner. I'll be the last one on the chain."

This had to work. He needed to get them all out safely and get back to his normal life—his home, his family. His breath caught as he thought about his mom and the last words he had said to her. There was no question. He was going to get back.

Everyone did as Ethan said. It was Brody holding on to the railing, then Maggie in front of him, then Ganna, Drake, Alyssa, and finally Ethan. Ethan reached out a hand to Jason, whose legs were pulled straight out in front of him in the air.

"Ohhhh boy," Jason said with a nervous laugh. "Am I glad I wore my tighter pants today. Otherwise, you'd all see my emoji underwear."

Ethan laughed and tried to get the picture of Jason in emoji boxer shorts out of his head. Yeah. That was definitely a sight nobody needed to see.

"C'mon." Ethan reached out his hand.

Jason hesitated. "I can't let you—"

"Look at me." Ethan was not going to let his friend disappear. "Let's do this."

Jason's face relaxed, then he nodded. "Let's do this!" He reached out and grabbed Ethan's hand while still remaining on top of Nith. Nith took advantage of the change and kicked himself free, but the pull of the cloud quickly pulled Nith toward it. In an effort to stop himself, he lunged at Jason. Nith grabbed hold of Jason's waist.

Ethan switched hands with Alyssa so he could turn and face Nith who had moved to the other side of the chain, with Jason moving with him. They stood in as straight of a line as possible and pushed at Nith. Jason dipped his lower body to the ground, tripping up Nith. Ethan pulled Jason back, which was just enough to pull him free from Nith.

"Now, Brody," Alyssa called.

Brody pulled everyone back.

Nith fought against the pull of the cloud as if he was walking against a strong, windy storm, but the pull was too much. It lifted Nith up in the air, pulling him closer and closer to the cloud. Nith's once powerful and intimidating figure looked small and frail against the blackness of the cloud. With one final tug, the cloud devoured him.

More and more things around them pulled into the cloud.

When every last object in The Keep disappeared, the room began to distort. It twisted and turned and crumbled like someone crushing a piece of paper. But it didn't stop there. The hallway connecting The Keep and the Castle suffered the same fate. Soon more rooms were pulled into the cloud. The maze whizzed by them as if it was a passing image, followed by the Grand Hall and the Shadow Room.

Meanwhile, Alyssa's ring grew warm in Ethan's hand as the cloud continued to slowly devour everything around them. He opened his hand and the ring floated up in the air. It hung there for a second.

Ethan snuck a peek at Alyssa, who had a look of horror and despair on her face. The pull of the cloud slowly pulled the ring, following Nith into its abyss. As if that were the final thing needed to seal the hole, it became less and less powerful. Instinctively, Ethan grabbed his sister's hand.

The friends held onto each other until, finally, the pull of the cloud ceased. Then there was silence . . . and darkness.

CHAPTER 30 - Home

Ethan's head was spinning, and the scene in front of him was blurry. "Wh–where are we?" He focused on the object in front of him until everything came into focus. It was a television. He glanced around. He was back in the familiar living room he had left so long ago. The kitchen was to the side of the living room like it always had been. He turned to Maggie, still holding her hand.

"Is–is it really over?" Maggie's eyes pleaded with him. He honestly didn't know. But it had to be. Nith was gone, so he nodded. "I think so."

"There you are." Their mom's familiar, angry voice echoed through the room. "Where have you two been?"

Ethan and Maggie looked at each other.

"With Alyssa, Brody, and Jason," Maggie answered.

Ethan looked at her sideways. Maggie shrugged.

He smiled to himself. It was true. He knew he would have to explain everything to his mom later, but it all was too overwhelming to even think about explaining what happened in a way that made sense.

Then he remembered how rudely he treated his mom before he disappeared. He couldn't get the image of the hurt expression on her face. And he didn't want to think about what may have happened to Gordy and Drake. One minute they were all together. The next minute they weren't. Would he ever see them again? He wasted the opportunity to make things right with his dad, and he lost him. He wasn't going to make that mistake with his mom.

He wiped a tear from his eye. He rushed over to her and hugged her, burying his face in her shoulder. "I'm sorry," he said in a muffled voice.

Mom's face softened, and she petted the back of his head. "I know."

A knock at the kitchen door interrupted their moment.

"It's open," Mom called.

Alyssa, Jason, and Brody stormed in. Jason's hair stood out in all directions. Ethan motioned to Jason to flatten his hair. Jason obliged, then ran over and grabbed Ethan and Maggie in a hug. "Oh, thank goodness you are okay."

Ethan and Maggie got a look from their mom.

Ethan quickly recovered. He nudged Jason. "What do you mean?" He eyed Jason. "We were together the whole time . . . right?"

Jason stepped back. "Pffft. Yeah. That's right." He looked at Ethan's mom. "Don't know what I was thinking."

Alyssa shook her head.

Brody stood there and slid his hand over his face. "Sorry," he mouthed to Ethan.

Ethan's mom looked directly at him. "Okay, well, we'll discuss this later. I have a meeting to get to. And if you go anywhere—" she stared at Ethan "—text me first!" She held up her phone.

Ethan nodded. "Deal."

After she left, they all breathed a sigh of relief. Ethan looked at Alyssa's finger and noticed the ring was still missing.

She frowned. "My ring, I know." Tears filled her eyes. "My grandmother's ring is gone."

Ethan's hung his head. He did it to her again. "I'm sorry. I didn't mean—"

Alyssa wiped her tears and grabbed his hand. "It's okay. If I had to lose my grandmother's ring, she would have wanted it to be because we helped somebody." She held Ethan's gaze. "And we helped a lot of people today."

Silence filled the room. Ethan squirmed. It was as if everyone was afraid to say anything about what happened—as if speaking it would make it more real.

Ethan cleared his throat. He needed to find out about Drake and Gordy. Were they okay? Where were they?

"So, anyone hear from Drake and Gordy?"

Silence.

Ethan's heart sank. He half expected Gordy to return to normal after Bailiwick was destroyed. It was destroyed, right? He rushed over to the gaming console and pulled up Seeker. The link was there, but it didn't work. The icon was a blacked-out image. A notice that read, "Currently unavailable," popped up on the screen. Yep. it looked like it was destroyed.

"Do you think they are gone?"" Ethan finally brought himself to ask.

"I don't know," Alyssa whispered. "They were part of the original game—like Nith. Maybe . . ." Her voice trailed off.

Ethan looked at Maggie. He wasn't sure how he felt about the fact that Gordy may be gone. On one hand, he had caused so much trouble, both throughout the game and in Nith's past. On the other hand, Ethan still felt that loss when he thought that Gordy might be gone for good. It was the same crushing feeling he had so long ago when his dad never returned home. The only difference was, his mom wasn't there to experience it this time. Yet.

He let out a deep breath. How in the world was he going to tell her about this? Saying,

"Oh, by the way, Mom, Dad never left us. The villain in the Seeker game kidnapped him as well as us. He worked with the villain, turned to our side, then was destroyed by Nith. Surprise," didn't seem like it was something she'd be able to believe, let alone process. And if Gordy was really gone, maybe it was better if she didn't know any of it.

Alyssa patted him on the shoulder. "I'm sorry. I shouldn't have said that. Are you okay?" She gave him a sympathetic look.

Ethan tried to find the words, but all he could come up with was a nod.

Alyssa grabbed his hand. "The hard part is over. And you know what? You survived."

He nodded again. "Thank you." He squeezed her hand and let it go.

She smiled in return.

When his friends left, Ethan made his way into the kitchen. Dishes were piled up in the sink and the counters were getting dirty. He checked the time: 5:15. Mom's meeting should be over in another hour.

"Hey, Mags, I'm going to clean up and cook some dinner for us."

Maggie's eyes widened. "Really?"

Ethan pulled out some ground beef, crushed tomatoes, garlic, and onions. He juggled it all and brought it to the counter.

"Yep." He frowned. "It's the least I could do. I was really

mean to Mom before we got trapped in the game."

Maggie lowered her eyes. "I know. I heard you guys that night. That's another reason why I was so mad at you that morning. She didn't see me, but I came out when you slammed the door. She wiped her eyes like she was crying."

Another wave of guilt twisted Ethan inside. "That's why I'm going to do more than apologize." He started chopping the onions and garlic. "I know I haven't helped much at all around here. That's going to change."

Maggie smiled at him. "Here, hand me the tomatoes. I'll get that started."

For the first time in a long time, Ethan and Maggie worked together, side by side—sister and brother. By the time their mom came back from her meeting, Ethan had set the table for the three of them and Maggie had plucked a rose from their rose garden in the backyard, which they used as a centerpiece.

"You guys did this for me?" Their mom's smile went from ear to ear. Soon they all sat down and ate dinner together, which hadn't happened in a long, long time. The only thing missing was their dad.

CHAPTER 31 - Max and Allie

Later that night, Ethan held his phone close to him. Alyssa, Brody, and Jason all agreed to check their Seeker game to see if theirs was gone too. If the game was really destroyed, then it should be destroyed for everyone, but that made him worry about something else. *If the game was destroyed, where are Drake, Ganna, and Dad?* He hadn't heard anything from any of them since they left Seeker.

He tried pushing the worries out of his mind. *Well,* he thought, *maybe I can check on Max.* He sent a text to Max.

"Hey. Are you there? It's Ethan."

Several minutes went by and he sighed, putting his phone away. Maybe Max was busy with something.

He decided to try Allie, but she didn't respond either.

No, Ethan thought as he twisted his wrists, *he had to have come back.*

He paced the floor, which let out a low creak when he passed the area that divided the kitchen and living room. He went over to his gaming console and checked for Seeker again. Nothing. The same message appeared that was there before.

"That's it," Ethan murmured. He texted Brody, Jason, and Alyssa to meet him at the corner of his block.

A few minutes later, all four headed to Max's house.

"Did you guys check Seeker at your house yet?"

Everyone nodded and confirmed that their games weren't functional either. That was a good sign.

After passing several blocks, they turned down Davidson Avenue and approached Max's house. Alyssa knocked on the door. A long, silent pause hung over them as they waited. Ethan's stomach twisted as the wait got longer. Max had to be back, even though Ethan had not actually run into Max in the Bailiwick Keep. Did Nith do something to him?

Finally, a lock clicked and the door pulled open. "Hey, guys." Allie motioned for them to come in. She definitely looked better than the last time Ethan saw her, and she actually had a smile on her face. Did that mean . . .

"In here." She motioned for them to follow her into the living room, where Max lay on the couch sleeping.

Brody's eyes moved from Max to Allie. "Is he . . ."

"Only sleeping," Allie said. "When he returned, he was really pale, but he was anxious when he realized he returned but you guys were still stuck in there."

Ethan let out a quick laugh. He could relate to that.

"We have been so worried," Alyssa said.

Jason pointed to Ethan. "Especially him. He was wringing his hands so much, I'm surprised they didn't fall off." He grinned. Then he patted Ethan's back. "But seriously, dude, you kicked butt today."

Ethan smiled. Jason really was a great friend. He vowed that he would be a better one to Jason. He deserved better than how Ethan had treated him. And the thing was, Jason's loyalty never changed, despite how Ethan responded. If that wasn't a true friend, he didn't know what was. And so, Ethan would be the good friend Jason and all his friends deserved.

Max stirred on the couch.

"Hey." Allie sat on a part of the cushion Max wasn't on. "You've got company."

Max lifted his head. He stared for a minute as he took in the scene in front of him. Then, he leapt off the couch. He went over and pulled them into one giant and crushing hug.

"Can't . . . breathe." Jason wiggled free.

"We were so scared you didn't make it out," Brody said after the hug broke apart.

"Me?" Max put his hand to his forehead. "You were the ones going head to head with Nith. When I got back, all I wanted to do was go back in and help you guys." He looked at Allie. "But Allie begged me not to, and after I told her what was happening, she felt that the fewer people you had to worry about, the better."

Allie nodded. "It sounded like you had your hands full. He wasn't going to listen to me. I know he wasn't." She gave him a stern look. "But then his parents found him, and that was the end of that."

Max nodded.

"It's fine," Brody said. "Everything worked out."

Ethan frowned. Well, almost everything. He still had no idea where Ganna, Drake, and Gordy went, or if they even made it.

* * *

The next morning, Ethan and his friends still hadn't heard anything about them. Ethan was starting to accept that maybe he'd never know. And if it was bad news, maybe he'd be better off not knowing. Or would he? There'd still be part of him missing. Could he really be okay not knowing whether his dad was alive or not?

But . . . wasn't that what he was doing to his mom? She had no idea about what really happened to her husband. Ethan sighed and went to find Maggie. He gently knocked on her bedroom door. She opened the door, hairbrush in hand, and let him inside. Maggie's usually wavy hair looked like she ran through a hurricane. She headed back over to her mirror.

Brush, brush, pullll.

He picked the middle spot of her bed and sat down. "I think we should tell Mom," he said.

Maggie put down her brush and faced Ethan. "Are you sure?"

He nodded.

"What about not wanting to worry or upset her?"

Ethan frowned. "I know I would want to know. She may not believe us, but we should at least try to tell her."

"Okay," Maggie said. "I'll meet you downstairs in five minutes." She pointed to her hair. "This is out of control today."

He grinned. "No kidding."

She threw a pillow at him as he ducked out the door.

He laughed and shook his head.

* * *

"You two aren't serious." Their mom placed her hands on the kitchen table. She looked around the table at Ethan and Maggie.

They nodded.

"You want me to believe that Aiden—your dad—was abducted by my ex-boyfriend, turned into a gnome, and is now missing?" She laughed. "You two and your stories."

Ethan coughed. "That's where we've been when you were looking for us." He wrung his hands, then stopped when he realized it. "Brody, Alyssa, and Jason were there too. They saw everything. And Max," he pointed out to her. She knew Max had been missing. "Max returned yesterday. He was there too."

She shook her head and stood. "Okay. I think I've heard enough of your story today." She turned to walk away, then turned back to them. "But it was cute."

Ethan and Maggie looked at each other. Ethan's jaw dropped open in shock. *Cute*? What they lived through was anything but *cute*.

Maggie touched his arm. "It's okay. She's never going to believe us. I mean, it does sound ridiculous."

Ethan couldn't argue with that, but that reminded him of Seeker. Where was everyone else? Drake? Ganna? Gordy? His heart dropped. He just got his dad back. Why wasn't he there with them? If the game was really gone, what happened to them? "Do you think the game is gone for everyone?" he asked.

"Probably." Maggie examined her fingernails. "All of ours were."

"I'm going to make sure." He picked up his phone and did an internet search. He typed, "What happened to Seeker?"

Several results popped up with headlines like: "Seeker goes Dark," "Seeker Ceases to Work—Rendering the Expensive Transport Useless," and "Seeker Crashes—Ronald Tinim Unavailable for Comment."

It sure looked to Ethan like Seeker was dead. When he went to put his phone down, he saw a notification blinking. He slid his finger to unlock the screen and clicked on his Chatterbox app. A direct message appeared from the Seeker profile. *That's odd,* he thought. *Isn't the game dead?* He looked up as Maggie sat down next to him on the couch. "Whatcha got there?" she asked.

"A message from Seeker," Ethan said, his finger hovering over the *View Message* button. He took a deep breath and then opened the message. It read:

Ethan and Maggie,

If you're reading this message, then I know you got back safely. I'm with Ganna and Drake, helping them get back home. I hope to see you soon.

—Dad (a.k.a. Gordy)

He breathed a sigh of relief. Everyone was safe. They did it. They actually stopped Nith from keeping the souls and merging the real world with the digital. As Ethan looked back on his adventure in Bailiwick, he was glad it was over, but he was grateful for the revived relationships and new friendships it brought. One thing was certain. He looked at Maggie and smiled. She smiled back. He was never going to take his family for granted again.

About the Author

Jennifer Gladen is a teacher and a children's author who lives and writes in PA. She uses her parenting and teaching experiences to create compelling and purposeful stories. She was born in Troy, MI but grew up in Philadelphia PA. She now resides in the Lehigh Valley in PA with her husband and children.

You can connect with me on:

- https://www.jengladen.com
- https://twitter.com/JenGl
- https://www.facebook.com/jengladen

Subscribe to my newsletter:

- https://mailchi.mp/c66f1ad15738/readers

Made in the USA
Middletown, DE
22 May 2021